Lady Justice and the Cruise Ship
Murders...another home run for Thornhill

Being a fan of other novels in Robert Thornhill's *Lady Justice* Series, I was eager to jump into this new offering. Thornhill, in his usual creative manner, has woven yet another witty murder mystery. In this work, we find Walt Williams, one of Kansas City's finest, back at it again.

On the heels of the unbelievable capture of a serial rapist, Walt, his wife, his partner (Ox) and Ox's new wife, all head on a much-deserved adventure (and honeymoon). This time, they move offshore to enjoy an excursion on an Alaskan Cruise line.

On a separate (but simultaneously connected trip) they are joined by attorney, Mark Stewart and his wife. They, too, are embarking on an adventure. A prominent archeological professor, eager to locate the long lost gold of Mark's ancestors, has contacted Mark—believing he has been successful in locating the treasure. Mark, a skeptic by nature, agrees to make the trip regardless of the outcome.

We find Walt and his crew on offshore games of cat and mouse, bait and switch, and the search for lost prospector's gold. Spinning its way through email account hacking, warding off revenge from newly released inmates and salmon bakes—this contribution continues to offer the clever capers we've come to enjoy from Thornhill.

Through wonderfully interlaced complications and unexpected outcomes, *Lady Justice and the Cruise Ship Murders* easily joins its series predecessors as equally funny and uniquely entertaining.

Kudos, again, to Thornhill on his latest series addition!

Avis Jenkins, Article Write Up

There's something about a murder mystery aboard a ship at sea...the culprit can't escape easily; but neither can the intended victim. Writers like Agatha Christie and Ian Fleming have used this vehicle to set up plots and sub-plots to make the reader roll with the waves as they sort through events and clues. Robert Thornhill skillfully brings this setting into the world of Walt Williams as he presents us with mystery/comedy #11, *LADY JUSTICE AND THE CRUISE SHIP MURDERS*.

The story unfolds as Walt Williams, retired real estate agent, now a member of the Kansas City Police Force's City Retired Action Patrol (C.R.A.P.), and his wife, Maggie, have been invited to join Walt's partner Ox, and Ox's policewoman wife, Judy, on their honeymoon. The decision is to take a weeklong Alaskan cruise that includes panning for gold (Ox's dream) and a salmon bake for Judy.

With Thornhill's skill of interweaving story lines, we learn that another couple from KC is also headed to Alaska to hopefully retrieve a hidden treasure trove of gold. The plot thickens when a murder is committed on the first night aboard the ship right down the hall from Walt's room. Continuous action will hold the reader's attention, but Thornhill also provides moments of prose about the beauty of Alaska and humorous events that occur on the ship. Finally, the culprits are caught and Lady Justice triumphs once again. This is a pure fun and entertainment...keeps you turning the pages until it's done!

Christina Fullerton-Jones, Independence, MO.

Robert Thornhill hits the mark again in *Lady Justice And The Cruise Ship Murders.*

Walt and Maggie accompany Ox & Judy on their honeymoon cruise to Alaska. Once on board, two people end up dead, and it looks like a case of mistaken identity. Another couple's life is in danger if Walt and gang can't catch the murderer first.

Fantastic read, with a bit of Alaskan history and great photos. A must read for mystery lovers.

Sheri Wilkinson, Goodreads

LADY JUSTICE

AND THE

CRUISE SHIP MURDERS

**A WALT WILLIAMS
MYSTERY/COMEDY NOVEL**

ROBERT THORNHILL

Lady Justice and the Cruise Ship Murders
Copyright October, 2012 by Robert Thornhill
All rights reserved.

This novel is a work of fiction. Names, incidents and entities included in the story are products of the author's imagination. Any resemblance to actual persons, events and entities is entirely coincidental.

Published in the United States of America

Cover design by Peg Thornhill
1. Fiction, Humorous
2. Fiction, Mystery & Detective, General

DEDICATION

Peg and I would like to thank the Captain and crew of the Statendam for making our first Alaskan Cruise a memorable one.

Our cruise and our shore excursions were used as the foundation for *Lady Justice and the Cruise Ship Murders.*

While many of Walt's adventures were based on our own personal experience, this is obviously a work of fiction.

Although the ship, the ports and the places we visited are real, the story itself is a product of my warped imagination.

Also, while much of the historical content is accurate, I must admit that some facts were altered to fit the plot.

With all that being said, Peg and I have returned to Missouri with a much deeper appreciation of our northernmost state, its citizens and its colorful history.

LADY JUSTICE
AND THE
CRUISE SHIP MURDERS

PROLOGUE

Mark Stewart examined the postmark on the letter that his wife, Amy, had handed to him when he arrived home from work.

"Skagway, Alaska," he muttered. "We don't know anyone in Alaska, do we?"

"Not that I know of," she replied. "Maybe if you opened it instead of just staring at it, you would find out who sent it."

Mark, a junior partner in a Kansas City law firm, was the cautious one in the family. Amy was the more adventurous of the two.

Mark tore open the envelope and pulled out a letter that had been neatly typed.

Dear Mr. Stewart,

By way of introduction, let it suffice to say for now, that I am a historian and amateur archeologist in Skagway, Alaska.

My studies have led me to some documents that are linked to your great-great grandfather, John D. Stewart, a prospector during the Alaskan Gold Rush.*

---

* See photo, page 215

Your great-great-grandfather arrived in Skagway in July of 1898 bearing a bag of gold weighing nearly fifteen pounds.

The gold was taken from him by two men that were part of Jefferson (Soapy) Smith's gang of con men.*

It was this theft that led to the demise of Soapy Smith in the infamous shootout on Juneau Wharf.

During the melee that followed Smith's death, your great-great grandfather's gold was never recovered and it was assumed that it had been hidden away by Slim-Jim Foster and John Bowers, the con artists that had taken it from him and who were arrested shortly afterward.

My studies and the documents that I have found have given me clues as to the whereabouts of your great-great grandfather's gold.

You, of course, would be the rightful heir if the gold does indeed still exist.

The gold would be worth in excess of seventy-five thousand dollars in today's market.

My interest is that of a scholar and should you be interested in joining me to locate your great-great-grandfather's legacy, I would only ask for the rights to the story of the discovery and a modest sum to cover my expenses.

---

*   See photo, page 215

I realize how preposterous this may sound, but I urge you to give it some thought. If you are interested in pursuing this quest with me, please respond by email to: prospector@ak.rr.com.

If I don't receive a reply within a month, I will assume you have no interest in the venture and I will pursue other means to locate your great-great grandfather's gold.

Sincerely,
A. Prospector.

Mark stared at the letter for just a moment before wadding it up and throwing it across the kitchen.

"Well that's a new one," he said with disgust. "I wonder if this jerk is related to the Nigerian guy that keeps trying to send me money on the Internet?"

Amy retrieved the wadded-up letter and smoothed it out on the countertop.

"Is this true?" she asked. "I mean the part about your great-great grandfather being a prospector in Alaska? I've never heard you talk about it."

"I heard stories from my grandfather when I was a kid, but the old guy told a lot of tall tales. I guess I just figured that this was another one."

"There's a lot of detail here," she said, reading the letter again.

"Amy!" he said sarcastically, "surely you don't think there's anything to this!"

"I don't know, but I think it's worth looking

into. It wouldn't cost anything to do some research of my own and he did give us a month to respond. Would it be okay with you if I did a little digging into your family's history?"

"Knock yourself out!"

CHAPTER 1

"There's gold in them thar hills," Ox, my partner in the Kansas City, Missouri Police Department, declared as he perused his searches on the Internet.

Ox had married Judy DeMarco, a fellow officer, just a month ago and he was like a kid in a candy store as he and Judy planned their honeymoon.

They had decided on an Alaskan Cruise and had invited me and Maggie, my wife of just over a year, to tag along.

At sixty-nine years of age, neither of us had been on a cruise, so I had to admit that we were pretty excited too.

Ox had been looking at the array of shore excursions that were available at the ports of Juneau, Ketchikan and Skagway.

"Look," he said with enthusiasm, "we can pan for gold! I always wanted to pan for gold!"

"You do realize that those places are just tourists traps?" I asked. "There hasn't been any gold in those old mines for years."

"Doesn't matter," he replied. "I just want to learn how to do it. I've read the stories of the old prospectors who braved temperatures of sixty below zero up in the Klondike searching for the one big strike. Alaska was the last great American frontier and those guys were tough as nails. I just want to relive a little bit of American history."

"Then by golly, we'll pan for gold," Judy

declared, "as long as we can do the wild salmon bake out on an open fire."

The sixty below zero got Maggie's attention. "Exactly when are you planning this cruise? I hope we're not going in the dead of winter."

"No, it's pretty harsh up there about nine months of the year," Ox replied, "so we're thinking the first of June."

"Great! Then we'll have a few months to get ready."

"Get ready? For what?" Ox asked. "We're just taking a little boat trip and doing some sightseeing."

Maggie and Judy exchanged looks. "Don't worry about it, Big Guy," Judy said smiling. "Maggie and I will take care of the details. All you boys have to do is jump when we say jump and do exactly what we tell you to do. Understand?" she asked jokingly.

Now Ox and I exchanged looks.

We understood perfectly.

"Have you decided on a cruise line?" I asked.

"Not for sure," Ox replied. "These Alaskan cruises are pretty pricey, so we've been looking for the best deal. Actually, that's what I want to talk to you about.

"We got this thing in the mail that says that if we attend a special presentation about vacations at the Drury Inn, they will give us a cruise --- for free --- and there's no obligation to buy anything! Even better, they said we could bring friends and they would get a free cruise too. Isn't that great?"

Now it was time for Maggie and I to exchange looks.

Maggie and I had been to Hawaii and to Branson and had been lured into timeshare presentations with offers of free luaus and dinner shows and, yes, even a cruise.

"Ox, haven't you ever heard the old saying, 'there's no such thing as a free lunch'?"

"Actually," Ox replied, there is going to be a buffet of appetizers --- all for free!"

"No, you're missing my point. They are offering all of this stuff to get you to buy into their vacation program. They're selling timeshares in fancy resorts, and they're very good at it."

Ox pulled the mailer out of his pocket. "No obligation. It says so right here. Judy and I are going," he said with conviction, "and we want you and Maggie to come with us."

I figured that we'd better go or Ox might end up owning a studio apartment in Fiji.

At the second shift squad meeting the next day, Captain Short had some disturbing news.

"There's been another incident on the Trolley Track Trail. This was not just another confrontation with the attacker demanding wallets and jewelry. A woman was brutally beaten and raped.

"She had been at The Well, a bar and grill at

74th Terrace and Wornall. She lives just a few blocks south on 78th Street and rather than drive, would walk the Trolley Trail to her home.

"The incident occurred about eleven last night. The woman described her attacker as a white male, close to six feet tall and weighing one hundred and eighty. He was wearing a ski mask.

"We need to canvass the area and see if anyone saw or heard anything. Your assignments are posted."

The Harry Wiggins Trolley Track Trail is nearly seven miles in length running from 85th and Prospect on the south to Volker Boulevard on the north.

As the name implies, the trail lies where the tracks of the old trolley cars took passengers from south Kansas City to the urban shopping districts.

It winds between Brookside, Main and Wornall Roads. Much of the trail runs adjacent to the backyards of residential neighborhoods but some of it runs straight through busy shopping districts lined with bars and fast food restaurants.

Dark wooded areas, away from lights and people, surround a few stretches of the trail. Most of the trail users know not to travel those areas after dark. However, pretty much any part of the trail, with the exception of the part through the shopping districts, could harbor an attacker after sundown.

Ox and I were to interview the patrons and staff at The Well.

Word of the attack had spread through the

Waldo community and people were on edge. No one is comfortable knowing that a rapist is roaming the streets of their neighborhood.

The woman that was attacked was a regular at the The Well.

A local band from just across the state line, The Stolen Winnebagos, had just finished their first set when the bartender saw her leave alone. As far as he knew, no one from the bar had followed her.

We questioned other patrons that had been at The Well the previous evening, but none of them had seen anything out of the ordinary.

We hoped that other officers canvassing the neighborhood had better luck because we had come up empty.

Ox was chomping at the bit to get to the Drury Inn. He just knew that before the evening was over, he would have his free cruise.

The four of us piled into his SUV and headed to the motel.

A bubbly young woman met us in the lobby and directed us to a meeting room where another comely lass took over.

She gave us information sheets to fill out and told us that when we had them completed, we could help ourselves to the buffet.

The form wanted us to reveal pretty much every detail of our financial history. I suppose they needed that to decide how much time they would spend 'helping' us come to a decision.

When the forms had been turned in, we headed to the buffet. This was an evening of our life we would never get back so I figured that we might as well make the most of it.

They had a big pot of little weenie things steaming in BBQ sauce, which was one of Ox's favorite treats. As I watched him fill his plate for the third time, it gave me a warm feeling knowing that he wouldn't be leaving empty handed. I didn't have high hopes for the cruise.

There were maybe twenty other couples attending. Some were young yuppie types, a few middle-agers and a lot of old farts like me. I guessed they were leaning heavily toward the group with the largest disposable income and the most free time to travel.

When most of the paper plates were empty, a guy that looked like a cross between a used car salesman and a lounge lizard picked up a mike and welcomed us all.

He had his banter down pat and ushered us into the wonderful world of vacation travel.

For twenty minutes, a huge screen on the wall behind him displayed slide after slide of exotic tropical wonderlands, lush golf courses and magnificent resorts.

Ox's eyes were glued to the screen and I

expected him to start drooling any minute.

When the last slide disappeared, the emcee began his close.

"All of these wonderful places can be yours, simply by enrolling in our vacation club."

I saw Ox's lips move silently, but I know he was asking, "How much?"

It turned out that one week per year could be ours for a mere $45,000 plus an annual maintenance fee of $585.00.

That was approximately Ox's annual salary.

I saw the disappointed look on my friend's face when he heard the news and I felt for the big guy.

After the presentation, a vacation club rep, whose job was to get our signatures on a contract, joined each couple. When we politely declined, we were told to hang on a moment, there just might be something they could do for us.

Another fellow, obviously one notch up the food chain, came by with the wonderful news that he had just a few foreclosures they had picked up and we could move right into one for just thirty grand.

Who could pass up a deal like that?

When we had both said 'no' for the fourth time around, they finally gave up and another gal brought us our 'thank you' gifts.

Sure enough, there was a cruise, not a seven day cruise to Alaska, but a three day cruise to the Bahamas, and certain restrictions would apply, one of them being that pretty much the whole year was blacked out except for the rainy season. The cruise was indeed free, but of course with the port fees, etc, etc, etc, the actual cost was pretty much the same as the cruises we had seen online.

Ox left the hotel that evening a disappointed but wiser man.

I considered reminding him again that there is no such thing as a free lunch, then I remembered the weenies.

CHAPTER 2

Amy knew that her husband was a skeptic by nature --- not a bad trait for an attorney, and that she would have to handle the situation delicately.

She had spent the better part of a week researching her husband's family tree at the Midwest Genealogy Center and had poured through dozens of accounts of the Alaskan gold rush era.

She had discovered that the information contained in the letter from A. Prospector had been accurate.

She knew that her husband dealt in facts not fantasy, so she had photocopied documents and presented them like one of his legal briefs.

She had decided to wait until after the evening meal when he was relaxed and had put the rigors of his daily grind behind him.

When she felt that the time was right, she was ready to make her case.

"Mark, I have something I would like to share with you."

He saw the letter on top of the stack of papers in her hand.

"Is this about that silly letter we received last week? I thought we were past that."

"You said you didn't object to me doing some digging, so I'd like to show you what I've found."

Mark reluctantly followed her to the kitchen table where she laid out her week's work.

When she had finished, he gave her a smile.

"Are you sure you're not an attorney? We may have to offer you a position. Now what, exactly, are you suggesting?"

"I think we should email the guy and see what he has in mind. What harm could it do? He already knows who we are and where we live. I'd love to hear what he has to say."

Mark thought it over. "I guess it couldn't hurt and you have done a lot of work --- okay, just for you."

They booted up the computer and typed:

Mr. A. Prospector,

We found your letter to be interesting and factual, at least on the surface.

While we make no promises or commitments at this point, we would be interested in hearing what you have in mind.

Sincerely,
Mark Stewart

Mark looked at his wife. "Good enough for now?"

She nodded and he punched 'send'.

They had just settled in for an evening of TV when the computer announced, "You have mail, Sir."

"That was fast," Mark said as they opened their Inbox.

Dear Mr. Stewart,

Thank you for your prompt reply.

As I mentioned in my letter, Slim-Jim Foster and John Bowers, the members of Soapy Smith's gang that stole your great-great grandfather's gold, were apprehended in the forest outside of Skagway on their way to the White Pass Trail.

The gold was not in their possession at the time of their capture, leading authorities to believe that it had been hidden away in the forest for retrieval at a later date.

Both men were incarcerated in Juneau, and it was during this period of incarceration that Foster made notes as to the location of the gold, lest he forget before his release.

Somehow, these notes were included in a box of artifacts that the prison released to the University of Alaska Southeast in Juneau, for historical purposes.

In my position at the University, I stumbled upon these old notes.

I'm sure, with your inquiring mind as a barrister, you are wondering why I don't just follow the clues and claim the gold for myself.

The foremost reason is my advanced age. Traipsing through the Alaskan forest is not an old man's game and I would be fearful to attempt such a quest alone.

Secondly, you are the rightful heir of John D. Stewart and have lawful claim to the gold, if indeed it *still exists.*

Lastly, as a scholar, I may have one last piece to publish as part of my legacy and I can think of no more exciting way to end my academic career than to discover a cache of gold hidden away for over a century.

If you will agree to come north, I will meet you in Skagway and we can commence this wonderful adventure together.

Now that we have established a line of communication, I will introduce myself.

Yours in adventure,

Alfred R. Quimby, PhD

Mark and Amy stared at the email, but neither of them spoke.

Amy punched some keys and 'Google' appeared on the screen. She typed the name, Alfred R. Quimby, and several references popped up immediately.

Most were excerpts from scholarly works about the history of Alaska.

"Looks like he's for real," she said. "What do you think?"

"Well, you know that I'm a born skeptic, but I am intrigued."

Seeing an opening, Amy forged ahead. "You know that we've been talking about getting away for a while. What better place than Alaska --- maybe even a cruise. This is a perfect opportunity to know more about your family history, but even if it turns out to be a bust, at least we've had a nice vacation. Whadda you say?"

"I say you present a very compelling case, counselor," he said with a smile. "Let's do it!"

After our disappointing evening with the timeshare bimbos, it was back to the Internet to search for legitimate cruise options.

Dozens of sites popped up, each one offering the very best cruises for the very lowest prices.

After a lot of digging, it appeared that a few cruise lines handled the bulk of the Alaskan cruises.

We said eennie meenie miney moe and picked the Holland-America Line.

There were so many options to choose from on their website, we quickly became confused and opted to speak to a travel professional.

A perky little gal named Lauren came on the line. We explained that we were beginning cruisers and had absolutely no idea what we were doing.

Evidently we weren't the first ignoramuses that she had dealt with. A half hour later, we were booked on our seven-day Alaskan cruise, and yes, Ox was going to pan for gold and Judy got her salmon bake. Maggie and I were just tickled to be invited along.

As soon as the phone was snapped shut, the first meeting of the Alaskan Cruise Women's Auxiliary Meeting was convened.

"So much to do!" Judy declared. "There's the wardrobe and ----"

"Wardrobe?" Ox asked. "What wardrobe?"

"The clothes we're going to take with us. There's four dressy casual evenings, two formal evenings, sportswear for around the ship, warm clothing for our excursions, raingear, and, of course, something special just for you. It *is* our honeymoon."

Ox was dumbfounded. "We're only going to be gone seven days!"

"Oh really, Mr. GQ," Judy replied, "and just what are you going to wear?"

"Pants --- shirts --- skivvies --- how hard can it be?"

Judy rolled her eyes. I think it was fortunate that Maggie was along so that she would have someone to commiserate with.

I, on the other hand, had to agree with Ox. How hard could it be?

I soon found out!

The Trolley Trail rapist had struck again.

This time it was a female student at the University of Missouri-Kansas City.

She lived at the Johnson Residence Hall on Oak Street. The south end of the Hall was just a hundred feet from the north end of the Trolley Trail.

She had hit the trail at five in the morning for a run before classes and was attacked a few blocks south of the campus.

At that early hour, there were no witnesses and we had no leads as to the identity of the attacker.

The captain called Ox, Judy and me into his office.

"We have to stop this guy," he said. "Residents living along the trail are afraid to leave their homes and trail usage has nearly come to a halt. It's time for a decoy operation and we think the three of you can handle it."

"What's the plan?" Ox asked.

"There's no way that we can cover the seven mile length of the trail, so instead of trying to guess where the creep is going to strike next, we'll bring him to us. That's where you come in, Judy. You're good-looking and you can handle yourself, so you'll be the perfect decoy.

"We know the guy has targeted someone from The Well, so we'll have you start spending time there and walking home just like the first victim. We can't have anyone too close or we'll spook the guy, so Ox will patrol Wornall in his cruiser and Walt will be on the trail on a bike. You'll be miked so the guys will know if he comes after you."

I raised my hand, "Bike? I don't have a bike and why me? Ox is a lot younger."

Ox gave me a dirty look.

"Ox weighs two-thirty and you're a buck fifty soaking wet. That's why. Don't worry about the bike. We'll supply one for you."

Ox stuck his tongue out at me, which I thought was pretty juvenile.

"Let's get this thing rolling," the captain said. "Judy, you start hanging around the bar. Ox and Walt need to familiarize themselves with the trail so that they can respond quickly when you need them. Ox will drive all the streets on both sides of the trail and Walt will bike the trail from one end to the other looking for possible danger zones. Get to it!"

I had heard the old saying many times, "It's like riding a bike. Once you learn, you'll never forget."

I hoped that was true. I hadn't ridden a bike for over fifty years.

The sleek two-wheeler that was given to me was a far cry from my last bike.

I remember when I got it. It was Christmas when I was about ten years old. I had wanted a BIG bike so bad I could taste it, and sure enough, on

Christmas morning a big red Schwinn sat under the Christmas tree.

I can remember riding down Wall Street with the cold December wind whipping through my hair. It was my first taste of real freedom and I can still feel that incredible exhilaration to this very day.

The tires on that Schwinn were twice as wide as the one that had been loaned to me. The loaner had a bazillion speeds and my old one had just one --- pedal hard.

I climbed on and, sure enough, it was like I had ridden just yesterday --- almost. The difference was that my body, which included my legs, calves and lungs were fifty years older.

Thankfully, the trail was relatively smooth with few hills.

After a few miles, I began to feel another uncomfortable sensation. I didn't remember the seats being so narrow and hard.

Mr. Winkie and the boys were taking quite a beating and the hard, pokey seat felt like Doc Johnson was giving me a prostate exam.

By the time I had ridden the seven mile trail, I was chaffed, winded and walking bow-legged.

Several days had passed without another attack from the Trolley Trail rapist.

Judy was becoming a regular at The Well. She had been propositioned six times and had downed so many cocktails she joking said that she would have to enroll in AA after the operation was over.

She had walked home each evening to an apartment that the Department had rented about ten blocks south of the bar.

I had dutifully followed several blocks behind on my trusty bike. By that time I had gone through a full tube of Preparation H.

On the fifth night of the operation, we checked our mikes and settled in for another long evening.

Just before eleven, Judy's voice came through my earbud, "I've had it for tonight. If I have to hear one more lame pick-up line, I'm gonna kill somebody."

I watched her leave the bar and head down the Trolley Trail. I waited until she had gone several blocks and was out of sight before I climbed on my bike and followed.

Everything was quiet along the trail except for Judy's soft humming as she walked along.

Suddenly, I was startled by Judy's shrill voice. "OH SHIT!"

I heard grunts and groans and the sound of something heavy hitting the ground.

I peddled as fast as my achy, sixty-nine year old legs would move. "Judy, talk to me. What's happening?"

I heard a groan, "It was him! I flipped him but he came down on top of my leg. I'm okay but I'm not moving very fast. He's heading back your way. He might be headed toward the old school."

"I'm on it. Ox, are you getting this?"

"On the way partner."

Just as I got to the edge of the old school yard, I saw a shadowy figure race across the playground.

"He's at the school," I said. "I'm going in."

The old Bingham Middle School at 76th and Wyandotte had been closed since 2002. With the city population moving to the suburbs and the resulting decline in student enrollment, the Kansas City School District had closed a dozen or more schools. Bingham was one of them.

I crossed the cracked asphalt pavement of the old playground where I had last seen our runner.

I shined my light toward the building and saw that a door was standing ajar.

It was black as pitch inside and I was glad I had my flashlight. I drew my weapon and advanced slowly down the hallway.

The old building was huge, at least two stories tall, and it probably had a basement. The guy could be hiding anywhere. I hoped that Ox and backup would be arriving soon.

I moved slowly, stopping at every classroom and shining my light into every corner.

The district was obviously using the old school for storage as each classroom was filled with old outdated computer terminals, rickety desks or kitchen equipment from home economics classes.

As I looked at the old stoves, I wondered how many cookies eager students had baked over the years.

The teachers hadn't even bothered to take the artwork off of the bulletin boards before abandoning the building and little Johnny's last fearsome dinosaur stared at me from across the room.

I had just reentered the hallway when someone slammed into me with the full weight of their body.

I hit the floor and my gun flew from my hand. I did manage to hold onto my flashlight.

I started to go for my gun, but I saw that the rapist was a lot closer to it than I was and he had the same idea.

At that moment, I decided that discretion was the better part of valor, so I took off down the hall.

I heard the guy grab my gun off of the floor and cock the hammer.

Incredibly, the thing that popped into my mind was the scene from the 1979 movie, *The Inlaws*, where Alan Arkin is trying to avoid a hail of bullets and Peter Falk yells, "Serpentine, Shel! Serpentine!"

I figured if it was good enough for Peter Falk, it was good enough for me, and I zigged just as the guy pulled the trigger, and thankfully, the bullet zagged.

I stumbled down the hall like a drunken

sailor, weaving from side to side. Even with the light, I was tripping over broken chairs and wastebaskets.

The rapist had the gun, but I had the flashlight and I heard him cussing a blue streak as he crashed into things, hot on my tail.

I turned a corner and saw big double doors standing wide open. I ran through them and found myself in the huge gymnasium.

I figured there had to be several exits from the place, but to my dismay, when I shined my light, boxes of books stacked almost to the ceiling had blocked all of the other exits.

There was only one way out and the guy with the gun was almost there.

I searched frantically for someplace to hide, but the big old gym was nearly empty except for those damn boxes.

Then I saw it and as soon as I saw it, I hated it.

A braided rope, an inch thick, hung from the ceiling to the floor.

When I was in high school, such a rope was the most fearsome object in the school for me.

I was a wiry kid, weighing barely a hundred pounds. I could run and I could tumble with the best of the class, but upper body strength just wasn't my thing. In P.E. class, the coach made each one of us climb a rope just like the one I was looking at. If you could climb it, you were cool. If you couldn't, you were a wimp.

I was a wimp.

I could get maybe ten feet off the ground, but I'd be stuck right there.

That was fifty years ago. I had no idea if I could even hold my own weight at my age.

I figured I'd better try. The rapist's footsteps were just outside the double doors.

I switched off the flashlight, stuck it in my pocket and grabbed the rope.

I pulled with all my strength and wrapped my leg around the rope the way I remembered the cool kids doing it.

I just had to get high enough and remain quiet enough that the guy wouldn't notice that I was hanging up in the air.

The guy entered the gym. "Might as well come out cop. This is my playpen and I know there's no other way out. I'll get you sooner or later."

I heard his footsteps coming closer.

I figured that I must be at least higher than his head, but in the dark, I had no idea.

My arms were beginning to ache and I didn't know how much longer I could hang on.

I heard the siren from Ox's cruiser in the distance and I held on tighter, hoping he would find us soon.

"I can hear you breathing, cop. I know you're here. Let's get this over with."

I hadn't realized that I was breathing that hard, but in the cavernous old gymnasium the sound must have been amplified.

As I heard his footsteps grow closer, I held

my breath, which made hanging on even more difficult.

I realized that I was going to either black out for lack of oxygen or lose my grip for lack of strength very soon --- neither of which held much promise.

It sounded like the rapist was very close and I decided that if I was going to go, I might as well go out on my own terms.

I gripped the rope as best I could with one hand and reached for the flashlight in my back pocket with the other.

I was out of breath, both of my arms ached and I could barely grip the flashlight.

I switched on the light and saw that the guy was right below me. I had climbed an amazing eight feet.

I let go and as I dropped, I took the one shot I had and swung the flashlight at the guy's head.

I felt the impact, the light went out, I hit the floor and my lights went out.

The next thing I knew, Ox was cradling me in his arms and gently smacking my face.

"Walt! Wake up! Are you okay?"

"What? --- Where? What happened?"

"You got him, partner. You got the Trolley Trail rapist."

My arms ached, my head hurt, my legs were tired and my crotch was chaffed, but I never felt better.

All in a day's work.

CHAPTER 3

With all of the hoopla of Ox's wedding, the preparations for the cruise and the long nights away stalking the Trolley Trail rapist, I had made one of the fundamental blunders of matrimonial bliss --- I had forgotten about our anniversary.

I didn't forget the actual event. That magic day, two years ago when Maggie and I recreated the wedding ceremony in Elvis' *Blue Hawaii* will be burned into my memory forever.

What I did forget was the actual day. Somehow the date was lost in the two weeks that we spent in the tropical paradise of Hawaii, and it just didn't seem that important.

Maggie remembered.

The captain had given me a couple of days off to lick my wounds and when I crawled out of bed the next day, Maggie had prepared a breakfast of pineapple, papaya and waffles slathered in coconut syrup, my favorite Hawaiian breakfast.

As soon as I saw the papaya, it hit me.

"Oh, Maggie, I'm so sorry ---"

"Shut up you big hero. I'm going to give you a pass this time, because I know that somewhere out there is a woman that won't be attacked because you did your job. I'm so proud of you."

"Still," I said apologetically, "I should have remembered."

"I remembered for both of us. If you're up to it, I have a special evening planned."

What could I say but, "Sure, what do you have in mind?"

"First, we're going to enjoy a wonderful dinner at the Bristol Seafood Grill downtown and then I got tickets for the Yanni concert at the Midland theatre."

"Sounds great!"

Actually, I would have preferred Mel's Diner, but this was Maggie's gig so I figured that I'd better play along.

I'm not much on fine dining, but I'll have to admit the seared Mahi Mahi was wonderful and brought back memories of our days on Maui.

Another plus was that they had my favorite key lime pie and I can't get that at Mel's.

After dinner we walked to the Midland Theatre a few blocks away, for the Yanni concert.

The Midland, built in 1927, was one of Kansas City's historic treasures and the inside concert hall was adorned with all kinds of cool stuff that I know absolutely nothing about, but is quite beautiful.

While my musical tastes lean toward 50's rock 'n' roll, Maggie and I had seen Yanni before and we both love his stirring orchestral compositions.

On this particular night, my battered body was definitely more responsive to the lilting melody of the beautiful *Nightingale*, than Little Richard's *Rip It Up*.

In fact, one of the hazards of my job is that I have to associate, on a daily basis, with the dregs of humankind.

Just a few months previous, we had ended a serial killer's reign of terror only after ten people were murdered and with my recent encounter with the Trolley Trail rapist, my opinion of my fellow man was at an all-time low.

One of the things that make Yanni's orchestra so special is that the musicians come from all over the world, Greece, Russia, China, England, Cuba and, of course, the USA.

As I sat and watched the men and women from these diverse cultures playing their instruments in perfect harmony, I was impressed with the fact that music is, indeed, the universal language.

At the end of the concert, Yanni spoke of his recent tour of the Far East where he had performed at the Kremlin in Russia, China, South Korea, Singapore and other exotic locations.

His message was that when we get right down to it, we're all not that much different. He quoted the astronauts in the International Space Station who say that when they look down at earth, they don't see the artificial boundaries and borders that men have created. They see one world occupied by mankind.

His final words before his last piece, was that his travels had taught him one thing --- people can accomplish anything when they work together for the common good, and that we should never --- never --- give up on the human spirit.

When the concert was over, my body still hurt like hell, but my faith in my fellow man was healed.

In the technology lab at the University of Alaska in Juneau, three figures huddled in front of a computer screen.

Louis French, an instructor in computer science, clapped his hands. "He did it! Quimby actually convinced the Stewarts to come to Alaska to search for gold!"

"Thanks to your ability to hack into the Professor's email account, we know about it," Gwen Larson replied.

"So what's the plan?" Luke Larson asked. "How are we going to proceed?"

"It would appear that our young treasure hunters are combining business with pleasure. They have booked a cruise from Vancouver to Seward with stopovers in Juneau, Skagway and Ketchikan. They are supposed to meet Quimby in Skagway.

"He has never met the Stewarts, so the two of you will be aboard that cruise ship. You'll take care of the Stewarts, dump their bodies overboard and become Mark and Amy Stewart. When the old fool leads them to the gold, you'll take care of him too and the gold will be ours to split."

"A cruise and a fortune in gold," Gwen said, approvingly. "Sounds like a plan to me!"

Vacations are supposed to be fun, but somehow getting ready for them isn't.

Ox soon discovered that jeans and a Grateful Dead T-shirt, his idea of 'dressy casual', didn't exactly coincide with what Judy had in mind.

Ox hadn't bought a new suit in years, so one whole day was spent dragging the big guy from store to store upgrading his wardrobe.

Fortunately, I had acquired some new threads just a year ago, compliments of the US Government, when I was undercover in a sting operation, so I got to skip most of the guy shopping.

Unfortunately, Maggie thought it was important to have me along on *her* shopping excursion because she valued my opinion.

I spent grueling hours sitting in the 'husband chair' just outside the fitting room while Maggie ran back and forth trying on various colors and sizes of the same garment.

After a few hours, I was brain dead and all of the clothes looked the same to me anyway.

Invariably, Maggie would ask, "Which do you think goes better with my complexion, the red or the blue?"

If I said 'red', she would usually wind up buying the blue one, so I never really figured out why she dragged me along.

I needed a new pair of casual slacks.

I go to the rack, find a 34 waist, 30 inseam, and it's a done deal.

How hard can it be?

The next obstacle was our luggage --- or lack thereof.

The last time that we used it was two years ago on our trip to Hawaii, and it was old then.

When I pulled them out of the storage closet, one had a missing wheel and the handle wouldn't collapse on another one. All of them looked like they had been through World War II.

"A little duct tape and they'll be good as new," I said.

I saw the look on Maggie's face and didn't bother hunting up the duct tape.

Another afternoon was spent luggage shopping.

Who knew there were so many different kinds? The same size bag could run from sixty bucks to over three hundred.

We went to four different department stores before we found just the right combination of quality and price.

Once we had decided on the brand, we had to choose a color.

I suggested black, so we bought red. I didn't actually give a rat's patootie one way or the other.

Once we booked our trip, we started getting emails from the cruise line offering answers to frequently asked questions and things we would need before boarding the ship.

One of the messages said to be sure to bring along our passports ---- passports?

Why would we need to have passports to go to Alaska? Isn't that one of our fifty states?

Because we start the trip in Vancouver and that's in Canada.

Judy was the only one of us with a passport, so the rest of us got busy giving Uncle Sam all the information he would need to keep track of us for the rest of our lives.

There were a million little details like raincoats and umbrellas. The toothpaste in my travel kit had hardened into concrete and we had to put stuff in little baggies so that the TSA guys at the airport wouldn't confiscate everything.

Another thing that we had to consider was whether or not to try to carry our weapons on the trip.

After doing some research, we discovered that in order to do so, we would have to enroll in a class and that not only the airlines, but the cruise ship line and Canada all had a different set of rules governing firearms.

We decided not to bother. After all, we were going on vacation and who needs to be packing heat on a vacation?

Maggie and I live on the third floor of a three-story apartment building that I own on Armour Boulevard.

My dad, Bernice, the current love of Dad's life, the Professor, Jerry the Joker and Willie, my good friend and maintenance man occupy the other units.

Dad, Bernice and the Professor are all octogenarians and Jerry and Willie are in their sixties.

I had some concerns about going off and leaving them to fend for themselves, but each one, after hearing of our upcoming trip, assured me that everything would be just fine.

When Maggie and I had been on our honeymoon in Hawaii two years ago, we had scheduled some repair work to be done in our absence. The contractor had discovered a dead body concealed in the wall of the old building. Weird things just seem to happen when the Captain is not at the helm of the ship.

Another concern was the Three Trails Hotel, the other building that I own. It's a flop house with twenty sleeping rooms that share four hall baths. Naturally, the clientele is limited to old retired guys on social security and the unemployed who work out of the day labor pool.

This derelict institution is managed by Mary Murphy, a seventy plus matron that rules the place with an iron hand and a white ash ball bat.

In the past two years, Mary had shot an intruder and clubbed an assassin to death, and that doesn't count the two tenants that were recently murdered by a serial killer or the religious fanatic that had rented a room to make bombs to blow up Kansas City.

In my wildest imagination, I couldn't guess what might be coming next, but I figured that it would probably come while we were at sea.

Mary assured me that she had everything under control, but I had my doubts.

My only comfort was in knowing that this rag-tag bunch of seniors did have a good track record when it came to handling the unexpected.

My dad, Willie and Mary had saved my skin several times, but I had to wonder how much these old codgers had left in the tank.

Sometimes you have to just have faith and forge ahead.

CHAPTER 4

Wanting to get the most out of our journey to Alaska, we decided to do some research on the ports of call that we would be visiting on our cruise.

We spent hours on the computer and even went to the Mid-Continent Library to check out a book that had been recommended, *The Floor of Heaven, A True Tail of the Last Frontier and the Yukon Gold Rush* by Howard Blum.

Our society is steeped in the lore of the wild and wooly west. Every kid growing up in America has had a cowboy hero.

When I was a kid, it was Roy Rogers, Gene Autry and Hopalong Cassidy. With the advent of television, Marshall Matt Dillon and The Rifleman wore the white hats. Clint Eastwood filled the big screen with *Pale Rider, High Plains Drifter* and *The Outlaw Josey Wales*.

Such was not the case with the Alaskan frontier, at least for me.

Until I read Blum's book, I had never heard of George Carmack and Skookum Jim, the two prospectors that are credited with the first gold discovery in the Yukon and the guys responsible for starting the Klondike Gold Rush.

Charlie Siringo was a Pinkerton detective whose exploits rivaled any of our old west lawmen and Jefferson Randolph (Soapy) Smith was undoubtedly one of the greatest con men ever.

With a gang of over 300 men, Soapy Smith

virtually ruled the town of Skagway. He made a fortune luring the returning prospectors into his saloon and brothel, and his cohorts separated many a man from his pouch of gold dust with their crooked card games.

We all knew about the hardships faced by the pioneers that headed west in the wagon trains, but until I read the book I never knew of the 'stampeders' that carried tons of supplies on their backs hundreds of miles up the icy trails to the gold fields.

We read and we studied, and the more we read, the more excited we all were to explore the vast lands of America's last frontier.

On the day before our departure, our gang decided that a 'Bon Voyage' party was in order. After all, it was the first cruise for all of us and it was also the official honeymoon for our newlyweds.

Dad ordered a cake from HyVee that was shaped like a ship and Mary made punch that she swore wasn't spiked, but I suspected differently.

Bernice, upon hearing that our itinerary included cruising through Glacier Bay, reminded us of the tragic events surrounding the Titanic and told us to tell the Captain to watch out for icebergs. I promised her that we would.

Jerry, as usual, had his monologue ready for the occasion.

"This being your honeymoon," he said, "reminds me of a story.

"Now I realize that the two of you have been --- uhhh --- intimate for quite a while, but my story is about a young couple on their honeymoon who were getting undressed together for the first time."

Ox figured what was coming and buried his face in his hands. Judy just rolled her eyes.

Jerry forged ahead. "The man took off his shoes and socks and his toes were all twisted and discolored. 'What happened to your feet?' his wife asked. 'I had a childhood disease called tolio.' 'Don't you mean polio?' ... 'No, tolio, it only affects the toes.' The man then removed his pants and revealed an awful-looking pair of knees. 'What happened to your knees?' she asked. 'Well, I also had kneesles.' 'Don't you mean measles?' 'No, kneesles, it only affects the knees.' The new bride seemed to be satisfied with this answer. As the undressing continued, her husband at last removed his underwear.
'Don't tell me,' she said.
'Let me guess... smallcox.'"

Dad roared with laughter. "smallcox! What a hoot! How about it Judy? Has Ox been afflicted with the dread disease?"

Humoring the old man, Judy just smiled, "No, Ox is just fine, but thanks for asking."

Bernice, as serious as a judge, put her hand on

Dad's shoulder. "John, I'm just so thankful that you never had that disease."

It was at that moment that I realized just how much I was looking forward to being a thousand miles away.

The next morning was a killer.

Our flight from Kansas City to Dallas was to leave at 7:10. After a plane change, we would arrive in Vancouver, BC at 1:30 in the afternoon and be whisked off to the ship for a five o'clock departure.

Everything had to run like clockwork or the big ship would sail without us.

Given the hour drive from our apartment to the Kansas City Inconvenient Airport, we figured that we ought to be on the road by 4:00 A.M.

I just don't do 4:00 A.M.

Our alarm blasted us out of bed at three in the friggin' morning and as I struggled out of bed, my head confirmed my suspicions that Mary's punch had indeed been spiked.

We showered, dressed and packed the last suitcase just as Ox pulled up in front of the building and honked.

Dad, the retired over-the-road- trucker, had insisted on driving us to the airport, thus saving us the long-term parking fees.

He was to drive us in Ox's SUV, the biggest vehicle among us.

I dragged our two enormous suitcases and two carry-ons from our third floor apartment to the street. When Ox popped the rear door, the back end was already filled with Ox and Judy's luggage.

After some strategic rearrangement, we were able to get our two suitcases in the back but the carry-ons just wouldn't fit.

I was about to suggest that we put them in the front seat next to Dad, when Bernice appeared. She had decided that she had better ride along to keep Dad awake on the drive home.

When all was said and done, one carry-on was in my lap and the other one was under my feet. It was a loooong ride to the airport.

At 5:00, we pulled up to the curb at Terminal C and unloaded under the watchful eye of the airport cop.

I had figured that at 5:00 A.M., there wouldn't be many passengers at the check-in line.

Wrong!

At least fifty people were lined up at the American Airlines counter and the line snaked back and forth four times.

We dutifully took our place in line with our luggage and inched forward at an agonizingly slow pace.

Judy, Maggie and I had regular luggage carry-ons, but I noticed that Ox had brought an old, obviously well used backpack.

He defended his decision, saying that he saw no reason to spend sixty bucks on a new carry-on when his old backpack would do just fine.

On the other side of the rope barrier that kept us in line, was a couple with a young boy that was obviously no happier about being up at that ungodly hour than I was. He fidgeted and squirmed and hung on the rope barrier. His mother tried valiantly to keep the kid in check, but he obviously had a mind of his own.

Seeing that he had an audience, he made a face and stuck out his tongue.

I silently thanked the Powers That Be that Maggie was well beyond the childbearing age.

By the time we had reached the counter, we had passed by the boy three times, and each time we passed, he managed to come up with a different ugly face.

My only hope was that he was not headed to Dallas.

After checking our luggage and receiving our boarding passes, we headed to Gate #7 where the TSA guys would have their way with us.

Maggie and I had gone through this ordeal two years ago when we went to Hawaii, but Ox had not flown since the September 11th disasters.

As we approached the check-in station, I figured I'd better give Ox a 'heads-up'.

"You know that you have to empty your pockets of everything and take off your shoes and your belt."

"My belt? You've got to be kidding me!"

"Let me go first. Just do what I do."

I had no idea that my helpful gesture would cause such turmoil.

We undressed, put our stuff in the tray and placed our carry-ons on the conveyor.

Maggie, Judy and I passed through the metal detector with no problem and were retrieving our stuff when I heard the TSA guy say to Ox, "Sir, please step over here. The computer randomly selects passengers for a more in-depth search and you're 'it'. It's just routine. Nothing to worry about. Which carry-on is yours?"

Ox pointed to the old backpack.

Ox was escorted to an area where he was asked to stand with his arms out to his side. A guy ran a wand over his entire body and patted him down while another TSA agent emptied everything out of his backpack and began swabbing the interior with a little cloth patch.

I noticed that with his arms extended and the patting of the agent, Ox's pants were riding lower and lower. The agent finished just in time for Ox to grab his trousers and avoid a wardrobe malfunction.

The agent with the backpack suddenly stiffened. "Call security!" "Sir, is anyone else traveling with you?"

Dumbfounded, Ox pointed in our direction.

Uniformed officers arrived and gathered us together. "All of you will need to come with us. Where are your carry-ons?"

The officers confiscated our bags and led us to a secure room.

"What's going on?" I asked.

"The TSA agent found traces of gunpowder in this man's backpack. We have to investigate."

"I --- I --- I can explain!" Ox muttered.

"I certainly hope so," the officer replied.

"I think I can clear this up," I offered. "Three of us are officers with the Kansas City, Missouri Police Department."

"I --- I --- carry my guns in that bag when I go to the firing range to qualify," Ox said with a grimace.

Judy broke in, "Call our Captain. It's Captain Short. Here's his number," she said handing him a slip of paper.

The man took the paper. "Stay here and don't move a muscle."

While the guy was making the call, other officers were tearing our carry-ons apart looking for more incriminating evidence.

Ten minutes later, he reappeared.

"Looks like you guys check out, so we're going to let you go."

He looked at Ox. "Don't fly much, do you?"

Ox shook his head.

When we were finally reunited with our bags, Judy punched Ox in the arm.

"Cheapskate! All of this because you wouldn't spend a few bucks for a new carry-on. As soon as we land, we're going shopping. Understand?"

"Yes, ma'am."

We returned to the gate area and found seats. It was still fifteen minutes until time to board.

A young couple was seated across from us.

The woman spoke, "Hi, we're Mark and Amy Stewart. We were right behind you when the officers took you away. Since you're back with us, I'm guessing that you're not terrorists. Isn't it just terrible what they put us through to fly these days?"

"Well, to ease your mind," Judy said, "we're actually police officers --- well, three of us are. They found gunpowder residue from Ox's service revolver in his backpack. That's what the fuss was all about."

"I suppose we should be thankful," Mark said. "If you were indeed terrorists, I would certainly have been happy that they caught you. Is your trip official police business?"

"Oh, heavens no," Maggie replied. "Ox and Judy were married a few months ago and they're taking an Alaskan cruise for their honeymoon and Walt and I are tagging along."

"Oh, how exciting," Amy said. "We're taking an Alaskan cruise too. What cruise line did you book with?"

"Holland-America," Maggie replied. "We're on the Statendam."

"Us too!" Amy said, clapping her hands. "We'll be on the same ship."

"Is this trip for any special occasion?" I asked, trying to be friendly since we would be spending a week with these folks.

Amy looked at her husband and I saw him give her a little frown.

"Uhhh, no. Nothing special. Mark is an attorney and he's had a pretty hectic schedule. We just needed to get away so he could unwind."

Just then the woman at the desk announced, "We will now begin boarding flight 1119 to Dallas."

After the first class and special needs people had boarded, we were surprised that our group was called next. We soon found out why --- they board from the back of the plane to the front.

Ox and Judy were in the very back row on one side of the aisle and Maggie and I were on the back row on the other side.

We had seen Mark and Amy as we passed through the first class section. Amy gave us a little finger wave as we made our way to the cheap seats.

We stowed our carry-ons and watched as the plane filled.

Ox leaned across the aisle and whispered. "At least we won't have far to walk to the john." Our seats backed up to the only two toilets in the cabin section.

I only weigh a buck fifty and I was already feeling cramped and claustrophobic. I could only imagine how Ox felt, pouring his 230 pounds into the tiny seat. Needless to say, some of Ox extended into the very narrow aisle.

I dug my book out of my carry-on and started reading to distract my attention from my feeling of entombment.

I got the creepy feeling that someone was staring at me. I looked at the seat just in front of me and saw the face of the kid we had encountered at the check-in line. When our eyes met, he grinned and stuck out his tongue. It was going to be a looooong trip to Dallas.

At last we were airborne and I figured that as long as the captain had the 'fasten seats belts' sign lit, I wouldn't have to looks at the kid's ugly faces.

After we had leveled off at our cruising altitude, the stewardesses --- oops --- I meant flight attendants --- started serving beverages. Once we had been served, the whole situation seemed to have improved --- but the peaceful moment didn't last long.

Soon, the morning coffee on top of the recently consumed beverages began to send signals to the bladders of our fellow passengers.

One by one they unbuckled and made their way to the bathrooms. As the line began to form, I did some quick math --- over a hundred passengers and two toilets. The odds were worse than at my Three Trails Hotel where only twenty rooms share four hall baths.

The aisle couldn't have been more than thirty inches wide, which was acceptable when the line was single file, but when someone came out of the can and headed back to their seat, the only way that the two could pass was for one of them to squeeze into the seat space of the passenger seated closest to the john --- and that was Ox and me!

Each time we heard a flush, we knew that someone would be sticking their butts in our face.

Some apologized, but most didn't give a damn.

A particularly robust woman was standing beside Ox when we heard the next flush. The man that emerged was every bit as large. When the two met, the woman was obliged to almost sit in Ox's lap in order to let the man pass.

Apparently, the strain of twisting into that awkward position was just too much for the woman's constitution and I heard the distinct sound of the woman breaking wind followed by a gasp and Ox muttering, "Good Lord!"

When wheels touched down in Dallas, I couldn't get off the plane fast enough.

CHAPTER 5

Thankfully, our flight from Dallas to Vancouver was uneventful.

The obnoxious kid and his family went in a different direction, which so far, was the highlight of my day.

At Vancouver, we were directed to customs where we were to present our newly acquired passports.

We fell in line behind Mark and Amy Stewart. They looked amazingly fresh for having been in transit for ten hours. I wondered if it was because of the age difference or the first class accommodations. Probably both.

Amy was a little bundle of excitement. "This is so fun!" she gushed.

"Easy for you to say," I thought. *"You have your own private powder room in first class."*

"Definitely an experience I'll remember for a long time," Ox replied.

I guessed there was a hidden meaning there.

After customs, we retrieved our luggage and followed the crowd to the street where huge busses were waiting to take us to the ship.

Before leaving home, we had printed luggage tags that had been imprinted with our ship's name and our room number.

The baggage handler took our bags and told us not to worry --- our bags would be in our room after we boarded.

It was about a twenty-minute trip from the airport to the dock.

When we stepped off of the bus, our mouths dropped open.

The Statendam was as big as two and a half football fields.

We had seen cruise ships on Maui, but they were anchored far off shore. Standing right beside one was a completely different sensation.

I felt like the country bumpkin that comes to the big city for the first time, craning his neck as he stares at the skyscrapers.

I discovered later on as I talked with some cruise veterans, that the Statendam, carrying just over 1,200 passengers was actually small compared to some of the newer ships. Apparently, there were behemoths out there sailing the seven seas that could accommodate three times that number.

We walked the gangway and were met by ship's officers impeccably dressed in white uniforms.

After giving our names, we were issued plastic cards on which all of our personal information was digitally recorded. These cards were not just our room keys. We would have to present them when going on and off the ship and they would serve as on-board credit cards as well.

We boarded on deck #5. Our card indicated that our room was #401, so naturally, I assumed that we should go to deck #4

I soon discovered that cruise ships don't number like hotels. Our room was on deck #6.

We stepped out of one elevator just as Mark and Amy Stewart stepped out of another one.

"Oh this is just fantastic!" Amy gushed. "What are the chances that we both came all of the way from Kansas City and our rooms are on the same deck? What are your room numbers?"

"We're 401 and Ox and Judy are 399."

"We're 415," Amy said, looking at her key card. "Maybe we'll be neighbors."

We followed the directions on the bulkheads and made our way down the narrow hall.

It turned out that Mark and Amy had the last room on the ocean side about six rooms past ours.

We knew the rooms were going to be pretty small, but I definitely wasn't prepared for what we found.

Everything was there that you would normally find in a hotel room, full bath, queen bed, closet and TV, but it was all in a space about a third the size.

We spent the next hour unpacking and sticking the stuff from our suitcases in every nook and cranny that we could find.

When our luggage was empty, there was just no place to put it, so I finally balanced one suitcase on the nightstand by the head of the bed and the other one on the back of the couch. We probably wouldn't be doing much entertaining.

We had just finished unpacking when an obnoxious buzzer rang throughout the ship announcing that it was time for the mandatory lifeboat drill.

Our deck, #6, was called the Lower Promenade Deck and our window looked out onto a wide wooden deck that ran around the entire ship. It was on this deck that the lifeboats were stored.

Our plastic card informed us that we were assigned to Lifeboat Station #9 which was almost right outside our window.

As we went down the hall, past the Stewart's room, I noticed that they could walk right out their door, walk about five steps to the door to the deck and another five steps to the ship's outer rail.

Pretty convenient.

After the lifeboat drill, we huddled together to make plans for the evening --- or rather I should say that Maggie and Judy made plans for the evening --- Ox and I didn't have a vote.

The evening was to begin with supper --- no, wait --- supper is when ordinary people sit down to a hamburger and French fries. Our evening was to begin with dinner --- that's what you call it when it's fancy.

We had opted for 'open dining', which meant that we could eat at any time either of the two ship's restaurants were open.

We had two choices --- the Lido Restaurant, which for all intents and purposes was like a Golden Corral. There was a huge buffet line where you could walk through and select pretty much anything you wanted from Jell-o to roast beef. The other choice was the Rotterdam Dining Room where you were seated at tables adorned with crisp white cloths, cloth napkins, wine glasses and enough cutlery to last three meals. Waiters in starched white uniforms were there to cater to your every need.

Guess which restaurant the ladies chose.

We were informed early on that the Rotterdam was to be our venue of choice throughout the cruise.

Back home, my favorite eatery is Mel's Diner and Ox is partial to Denny's.

Judy had reminded Ox that in deference to his palate, she had suffered through enumerable Grand Slam's and that he owed her --- big time!

Maggie had just given me the 'evil eye' and a "What she said!"

In truth, we didn't have a leg to stand on, so we resigned ourselves to a week of 'fine dining'.

I dutifully changed from my comfy jeans into my 'dressy casual' attire and we headed to the Rotterdam.

The Maitre'd asked if we wanted two tables for two or if we wished to sit together. We, of course, wanted to sit together, so we were escorted to a table for six. For some reason, there were tables for two and tables for six, but no tables for four. It looked like another couple would be joining us.

Two waiters were at the table immediately to pull the chairs out for the ladies and when we were all seated, proceeded to drape our napkins across our laps.

I leaned over and whispered to Ox, "You

don't get that at Denny's."

The guy that was obviously in charge introduced himself, "I am Den and this is Mukti. We will be serving you this evening." *

Den presented us with menus while Mukti filled our water glasses.

As soon as I read the words at the top of the menu, I knew that Ox and I were in trouble.

Tonight's Featured Chef, Marcus Samuelsson Blending culture and artistic excellence, Marcus Samuelsson has won numerous awards as one of "The Great Chefs of America" by the Culinary Institute of America. Born in Ethiopia and raised by adoptive parents in Sweden, Samuelsson's cookbooks connect contrasting geographies and palates.

The menu itself confirmed my worst fears.

Appetizers
Summer Fruit Salad with Sambuca
Italian favorite, macedoine of fruits marinated in a sweet, Sambuca-flavored dressing

Carpaccio of Beef Tenderloin
Razor-thin slices drizzled with fruity olive oil, topped with shaved Reggiano-Parmigiano cheese and accompanied with a robust whole grain mustard sauce.

---

* See photo on page 216

Soups and Salad
Asian Chicken Consomme
Flavors of soy, coconut, lemon grass, ginger, and cardamom garnished with bean sprouts, diced chicken, water chestnuts, carrots, bamboo shoots and scallions

Chilled Watermelon Gazpacho
Delicately sliced watermelon swirled in a lemon sorbet and topped with lime leaves

Entrees
Filet of Beef Wellington
Mouthwatering tenderloin of beef topped with a duxelles of duck liver and mushrooms, wrapped in a puff pastry, served on a mirror of Madiera sauce with duchess potatoes and a medley of green asparagus and Chinese pea pods

Quail with Apricot Bread Stuffing
Tender quail stuffed with Grand Marnier-scented apricot breading, served on a port wine reduction with Savoy cabbage, roasted potatoes and cherry tomatoes

At the bottom of the menu was the chef's recommendation for the perfect wine to accompany our meal.

Laboure Roi Pouilly Fuisse, France $54.00

As I read the thing, images of a half-pound burger and onions sizzling in melted butter on Mel's grill filled my mind.

The image was quickly replaced by Dorothy's famous quote from *The Wizard of Oz*, "Toto, I've a feeling we're not in Kansas anymore."

I glanced at Ox who was obviously in a menu-induced stupor.

"See anything you like?" I asked.

"What *IS* this stuff?" he whispered.

"Not a clue," I replied. "I'm afraid you're on your own."

Our wives, by way of contrast, were absolutely giddy.

At that moment, Den arrived at our table to take our orders.

Ox leaned over again, "What should we do?" he asked.

"I don't know --- maybe the Beef Wellington --- beef and potatoes can't be all that bad."

Ox and I ordered the beef and our wives ordered the quail.

As soon as Den left with our orders, another man appeared at our table.

"My name is Alex and I'm your wine steward. Would you care for wine with your meal?"

I remembered the Pouilly Fuisse stuff from France at fifty-four bucks a bottle. I glanced at Maggie and she gave me a little headshake.

"No thanks. We'll pass," I replied

Ox got the same message from Judy.

"Me, too," he said.

Then I had an inspiration that later I would regret when Maggie got me back in the cabin. "Alex, by any chance would you have Arbor Mist on your list?"

Alex looked bewildered.

"Peach Chardonnay, if you have it."

"I don't believe I'm familiar with that vintage, sir," he replied.

"Well you should check it out. You can get it at Wal-Mart for about four bucks."

"WALT!" Maggie could see that I was baiting the poor guy.

Alex just shrugged his shoulders and walked away.

I'm sure he was thinking, "*Bumpkins!*"

Mufti arrived with a basket of assorted breads and a tray of butter pats. Ox and I helped ourselves, just in case the Beef Wellington wasn't as advertised.

About that time, the young man that had escorted us to our table arrived with another couple that appeared to be somewhere in their seventies.

After being seated and draped, the woman spoke, "Good evening. I'm Irene and this is Paul. We're from Sun City, Arizona. What about you folks?"

"I'm Maggie and this is my husband, Walt," Maggie said pointing across the table, "and these are our friends, Ox and Judy. We're all from Kansas City."

"Oh, my," Irene said, feigning surprise.

I guessed that she had never met anyone named 'Ox'.

Sensing the awkward moment, Judy jumped in. "Actually my husband's name is George. Everyone just calls him Ox because ---."

There was really no appropriate answer.

"Really? How quaint!" Irene responded. "Is this your first cruise?"

Maggie nodded, "Yes, the first for all of us."

"This is our fourteenth," Irene said proudly. "Let me just share some of our experiences with you."

Out of the corner of my eye, I saw Paul roll *HIS* eyes and slump down in his seat.

"Our first was to the Caribbean, and let me tell you -----."

By the time our entrees arrived, Irene was on cruise #7.

Ox leaned over and whispered, "What's the protocol here? Are we supposed to care about all this?"

Judy must have read his lips, because she gave him 'the look'.

Den placed our plates in front of us, but Irene never skipped a beat. "Our eighth cruise to Europe was undoubtedly the best --- blah, blah, blah."

I tuned Irene out and focused my attention to Chef Samuelsson's dinner creation.

Four sprigs of asparagus and about as many pea pods surrounded a thing that resembled a crème puff. Under it all was some dark, gooey stuff. I figured that must be the Madiera sauce.

I heard Ox mutter, "I thought there was supposed to be potatoes."

Judy whispered, "They're under your beef."

Ox slipped the crème puff to the side, revealing a dollop of white stuff. "This just isn't right."

I did the same and tasted the potatoes. They actually weren't half bad, but there were only two bites.

"Try them," I said. "They're pretty good."

It didn't take Ox long to finish off the potatoes and he proceeded to attack the Beef Wellington.

He removed the top layer of pastry revealing a gray paste on top of the beef. He looked questioningly at Judy.

"That's the duck liver duxelle," she whispered.

I thought that Ox was going to loose his potatoes right there.

I tried the asparagus and the pea pods. They were both crunchy. I'm sorry --- some things are just ingrained in my psyche --- cooked vegetables are supposed to be soft and soup is supposed to be hot.

Meanwhile, Judy and Maggie were ooohing and ahhhing over their apricot quail.

Den stopped by and asked how we were enjoying our meal.

I handed him the empty breadbasket and

asked if we could have a refill.

Irene had just finished with her narrative of their trip through the Panama Canal when their entrees arrived. The one good thing about the Beef Wellington was that Irene couldn't talk while she was chewing.

Den removed our plates and offered the dessert menu.

Coconut Rice Pudding
Baked with raisins, ginger, lemon grass, and vanilla bean, served chilled with a slice of fried pineapple

Den had obviously seen that Ox and I had barely touched our plates. Seeing our downcast look as we checked out the dessert, he gave us a knowing smile. "I think I might be able to find a hot fudge sundae or two if you would prefer."

I momentarily feared that Ox was going to leap to his feet and hug the guy.

"Would you care for coffee with your dessert?"

"Indeed we would."

Den proved to be a real jewel. Over the course of the meal, we had learned that he and Mukti, as well as most of the dining room waiters, were from Indonesia.

He told us that of the 530-crew members, over half were Filipino and most of the rest were from his country.

We polished off our dessert and coffee and

rose to leave, but Irene wasn't quite finished with us yet.

"We've so enjoyed sharing dinner with all of you, but I have so much more to tell you. Maybe we can sit together again and I call tell you about our trip to the Mexican Riviera. Wouldn't that be fabulous, Paul?"

"Yes, Dear."

Reflecting back, I think those were the only words poor Paul had uttered all evening.

"Maybe so," Maggie said sweetly.

"Not a snowball's chance in hell," I whispered as we walked away.

"Shhhhhh! She'll hear you!"

It was about a quarter to seven by the time we reached our cabins. Our next activity was the Captain's Welcome Party in the ship's huge theatre. I was totally exhausted from our trip and was anticipating an hour of just doing nothing.

I had just kicked off my shoes when the phone rang.

I looked questioningly at Maggie. She just shrugged her shoulders.

I picked up the phone and heard Ox's hushed voice, "Can you get away for a few minutes by yourself?"

I looked and Maggie was in the bathroom doing whatever it is that women do when they 'freshen up'.

"I think so. Hang on. Maggie, it's Ox. He'd like to walk around the deck a few minutes and get some air. Okay with you?"

"Sure, but be back here no later than seven-thirty. We want to get good seats."

"Good to go, Ox. I'll stop by your room."

Ox was in the hall by the time I got to his room.

"We have to hurry," he said. "I have to be back my seven-thirty."

"Me, too. Where are we going?"

"Just follow me. You can thank me later."

The elevator opened onto the Lido deck and Ox ushered me into the big buffet room.

"Walt, I'm starving!"

I had to admit that Chef Samuelsson had left me wanting more.

We made our way to the sandwich station and both ordered grilled turkey and cheese Panini's and topped them off with big slices of chocolate cake.

At seven twenty-five, we stepped off of the elevator on deck #6.

"Don't forget to brush your teeth," Ox warned. "We don't want the girls smelling turkey on our breath."

As I headed to our room, I had a momentary pang of guilt, but I got over it.

The Captain's Party was a smash. We were introduced to the crew as well as the five-piece band and the singers and dancers that would be entertaining us each evening for the next week.

We returned to our cabin, and in our absence, the room steward had turned down our bed, placed a little dog made of washcloths on the foot beside two pieces of luscious chocolate.

At nine-thirty, we crawled in bed. The last number that the band had played was running through my head. As my sweetie crawled in beside me, I burped the last remnants of the chocolate cake and felt the gentle rocking of the ship as it sailed northward. Maybe this was going to be a great trip after all.

At three-thirty in the morning, two figures silently slipped out of room #331.

At that hour, all was quiet and not a soul was stirring.

Luke and Gwen Larson padded down the hall until they reached room #415.

Gwen checked around the corner and seeing no one, nodded to Luke.

He pulled a device from under his jacket and inserted the card that was attached by a wire into the card slot on the door of room #415.

The device, supplied to them by Louis French from the University Technology Lab, whirred briefly. There was a small 'click' and a green light appeared.

Luke looked at Gwen who had stepped up beside him. "Ready?" he whispered.

She nodded.

They both removed hunting knives from sheaths attached to their belts and slipped into the room.

In the ambient light coming through the curtain from the deck outside, they saw the two sleeping figures.

It took but a moment for them to slip on either side of the bed and simultaneously plunge their knives into their sleeping victims.

The woman cried out, but Gwen pressed her hand against her mouth and plunged the knife again.

When both bodies were still, they pulled the covers back and wrapped the limp figures in the terry robes with the Holland-American emblem that the ship had provided to each passenger.

Gwen cracked the door open and looked up and down the hallway. Seeing no one, she returned and the two of them grabbed the first body, carried it around the corner, out onto the deck and pitched it over the rail.

The splash as it hit the water could barely be heard and with the ship cruising at 15 knots, the body was soon out of sight.

They returned for the second body, and in less than five minutes, the occupants of cabin #415 were but tiny dots on the open sea as the Statendam steamed ahead.

They returned to the cabin, wiped the blood off of their knives and pocketed the plastic room cards lying on the dresser. After a quick look into the deserted hall, they pulled the door closed behind them. "One step closer to a fortune in gold," Luke whispered as they crept quietly back to their cabin.

CHAPTER 6

Day #1 at Sea-Cruising the Inside Passage

When I awoke, I was disorientated. I knew that I wasn't at home, but nothing around me was familiar. Then I felt the gentle rocking of the ship as it plied the waters of the Inside Passage. I was actually on a cruise!

Mr. Winkie was standing at attention in response to the message being sent by Mr. Bladder.

I looked over at my sweet lady and her little snorts told me that she was still in la la land.

As quietly as possible, I slipped out of bed and into the tiny bathroom.

When Mr. Bladder was happy again, I donned the terry robe that the cruise line had provided, found my shoes amongst the clutter, plucked my room key off of the desk and silently slipped out the door.

On my way to the can, I had seen the lush landscape on the nearby shore through our cabin window. I figured that a brisk walk on the deck was just the ticket to get the old constitution revved up and ready for the day.

When I stepped into the hall, I saw the cabin steward staring at something on the carpet outside of room #415.

I was about to thank him for the chocolate he had left on our bed when I saw what had caught his attention --- a red splotch just outside the cabin door.

I knelt down beside him for a closer look and we both came to the same conclusion --- it was blood!

"I think you should check inside," I said, and he nodded in agreement.

He knocked. "Room steward," he announced.

When there was no response, he knocked again and announced a bit louder, "**Room steward!**"

He waited just a moment and when there was no response, he slipped his master key card into the slot.

After the gentle 'click' and the green light, he opened the door just a crack and peered in.

He jumped back and exclaimed, "**PANGINOON KO**!"

I had no idea what he had said, but the terror in his eyes needed no translation.

I pushed the door open and saw what had invoked his terror --- blood-soaked sheets on an empty bed.

People had obviously died in this room.

Then it occurred to me --- room #415 belonged to Mark and Amy Stewart!

I stepped back into the hall where the shocked steward had slumped to the floor.

"Call your security officer --- now!"

He pulled a walkie-talkie from his belt and rattled off some words into the mike. When he had finished, he listened intently and nodded. Then he said to me, "We wait here --- no go in."

I heartily agreed. We didn't want to

contaminate the crime scene.

Within minutes, two men came running down the hall.

The one obviously in charge looked at both of us. "Who are you?" he asked addressing me.

"My name is Walter Williams. I'm in cabin #401 --- and just so you know, I'm a police officer."

I could tell that he wished that I wasn't there.

"Wait right here!" he ordered, and slipped quietly into the room.

In a few moments he returned. "My name is Alejandro Reyes. I am the ship's security officer. We obviously have a situation here."

I nodded in agreement. "If there's any way that I can help ---."

He cut me off. "We have procedures in place for contingencies such as this. If you are indeed an officer, then you will understand what I must ask of you."

I nodded again.

"We are at sea and will not reach port until tomorrow. The last thing we need is for this incident to be spread throughout the ship. It could incite a panic that we could not control. I must ask you, as a professional courtesy, to keep this to yourself."

I assured him that I would.

"Very well then, please return to your cabin. We must process the scene before other passengers start milling about."

"Certainly," I replied. "Don't hesitate to call if ---."

He cut me off again, "Yes, of course. Now please return to your cabin."

I certainly understood. Back in K.C. it always took a squad of officers to keep the looky-loo's out of our hair while we were trying to do our job.

By the time I returned, Maggie was up and about. "Have a nice stroll, Bright Eyes?"

"Get your robe on while I call Ox and Judy. We need to talk."

Ten minutes later, the four of us were squeezed into our tiny cabin.

"What's going on down the hall?" Ox asked. "There's a half dozen people milling around Mark and Amy's room."

"That's what we need to talk about. I think they're both dead."

I told them what the steward and I had found and what Alejandro Reyes had told me.

Ox looked out of our window. "We're somewhere out at sea, so unless the perps jumped overboard, there's a killer with us on the Statendam."

"Sure looks that way," I said.

Suddenly, it looked like our peaceful cruise had become more than we had bargained for.

Although breakfast was being served in the fancy Rotterdam, Maggie and Judy agreed to let us eat at the buffet. In truth, the thought of our new friends being brutally murdered a mere fifty feet from where we slept had dampened our appetites. Mostly we just wanted coffee.

We climbed aboard the elevator and punched the button for deck 11.

When we entered the Lido, we were all shocked to see Mark and Amy Stewart wolfing down omelets and pastries.

As soon as they saw us, they waved. I'm sure they must have wondered about the expressions on our faces. It must have looked like we all had just seen ghosts.

They motioned for us to join them.

"We have some good news and some bad news," Amy said with a smile. "The bad news is that we're not neighbors anymore. The good news is that we had requested an upgrade and just after dinner last night we moved to cabin #169 on deck #9. We have a balcony now!"

"Fantastic!" Maggie said. "We're so excited for you."

Now the question that was running through our minds was, *"If Mark and Amy are still alive, whose blood was soaking the sheets in room #415?"*

We grabbed cups of steaming coffee and picked a table out of earshot of the other passengers.

"Now we have a real problem," Judy said. "Were the folks that were murdered in #415 the intended victims or did the perps think they were actually killing the Stewarts?"

"Good question," I responded. "Now the next question is whether we should tell the Stewarts."

"Well if it was my old room, I certainly would want to know," Maggie said.

"Do you think we can trust them to keep quiet?" Ox asked.

"Mark is an attorney. I would think he would know how to keep his mouth shut," I replied.

"Then let's do it," Judy said.

Mark and Amy were just finishing when we approached them.

"Good morning again," I said. "If you don't have other plans, I wonder if we could find a quiet place where the six of us could talk?"

"Well sure," Amy replied. "What about?"

I looked at the other passengers seated nearby. "I'd rather not say here."

Mark spoke up, "There's a library on deck #8. I'm guessing that there won't be many people there at this hour."

Mark was correct. The library was deserted. We found a curved couch facing the floor-to-ceiling windows that looked out on the sparkling water and the lush landscape in the distance.

The civilian-tourist part of me wanted to just curl up with my coffee and soak in the beauty, but the cop part of me wouldn't let that happen until I got to the bottom of this mystery.

When we were seated, Mark said, "Well here

we are. What's this all about?"

"Before we can tell you," I said, "you have to promise to keep this conversation absolutely confidential."

I could tell that I had his undivided attention.

"Certainly," he replied, "but why all of the cloak and dagger drama?"

"Because the people who took your old cabin last night were murdered."

Mark looked like I had slapped him in the face and Amy clutched her husband's arm in a death grip.

Mark quickly regained his composure. "Tell me what you know, please!"

I relayed my experience with the cabin steward and the security officer and what we had found in cabin #415. When I had finished, an ashen-faced Mark said, "I need a moment to talk to Amy. Will you excuse us?"

"Certainly. Take all the time you need."

We watched as the two of them went to the far corner of the library and engaged in an animated conversation.

"I think we struck a nerve," Ox observed. "I think they might have some insight into this incident."

"We'll know soon enough," Judy said, as the couple re-joined us on the couch.

"Did I recall correctly from our previous conversation that three of you are Kansas City Police officers?"

"Yes," I replied, "Ox, Judy and I are all on the force."

"Then under the circumstances, I --- we--- think that we have to trust you. Amy and I haven't been totally forthcoming with you about the reason for our trip to Alaska. When we explain, I think you'll understand why. Actually, Amy has done most of the research for our trip, so I'm going to let her tell the story."

We all turned our attention to Amy who was still reeling from our shocking news.

She took a deep breath and tried to compose herself.

"A --- a few months ago, we received a letter from an Alfred Quimby, a professor at the University of Alaska at Juneau. Based on his research and a document that had recently come into his possession, he believes that he has information as to the location of a cache of gold that was hidden away over a hundred years ago."

Now she certainly had our attention.

"Exactly why would he communicate this information to you?" Judy asked.

"Because the gold had belonged to John D. Stewart, Mark's great-great grandfather."

The significance of the name suddenly became clear to me. "As I recall from some reading we did before the cruise," I said, "John Stewart was the prospector that arrived in Skagway with a bag of gold that was subsequently taken from him by members of Soapy Smith's gang. It was that incident, reported to Frank Reid and the 101 Vigilantes, that led to the shoot-out on Juneau Wharf that killed both Reid and Soapy Smith."

"Very good, Walt," Mark said. "You've obviously done your homework. When Soapy was killed, the members of his gang knew that their grip on Skagway was over and they tried to flee from the Vigilantes. Slim-Jim Foster and John Bowers, the men that took my great-great grandfather's gold, headed north to the White Pass Trail. When they were caught, the gold was not in their possession. It was rumored that they had hidden it to be retrieved at a later date. As far as anyone knows, it was never recovered."

"So what makes this Professor Quimby think that he knows where it is?" Judy asked.

"Foster and Bowers were incarcerated at the prison in Juneau," Amy replied. "The prison just released some old documents that had been in storage for years to the University Historical Department. Quimby found something in those documents supposedly written by John Bowers that tells where the gold was hidden."

"So why tell you?" Ox asked. "Why doesn't Quimby just find the gold himself?"

"Apparently it's an age and health issue," Mark replied. "Quimby says that at his age, he's not interested in the money. He just wants to publish another historical work about the discovery before he dies. He also mentioned that he physically couldn't do the deed by himself. We're supposed to meet him in Skagway. He thinks that the gold is just north of town."

I was ready to ask the question that was on all of our minds. "Who knows about the real reason for your trip? Did you tell anyone?"

"Not a soul!" Mark declared.

"Someone on the Professor's end might have found out about the Professor's plan," Maggie offered. "How much gold are we talking about/"

"Quimby said that it would be worth about seventy-five grand in today's market," Mark replied.

"People have killed for a lot less," Ox observed. "The lure of gold has corrupted many a soul over the years."

"Have you and Quimby ever met --- in person --- or seen each other?" I asked.

"No," Amy replied. "We've only communicated by email. We Googled him and there were some old pictures of him when he was younger, but that's it."

"So, theoretically," I said, "if the two of you were taken out of the picture, and the two murderers were to meet Quimby in Skagway, he would never know the difference."

"Yes, I suppose that would be true," Mark said, "and the poor people that were killed last night in #415 were supposed to be us!"

"That's certainly a possibility," Judy replied.

Suddenly the color drained from Amy's face. "Then that means that there are two killers aboard this ship and when they discover that we're still alive, they might try again!"

"If our theory is correct, then yes," I said. "They might try again."

With trembling lips, an obviously shaken Amy looked at each of us and asked, "Can you help us?"

When our little gathering broke up and we headed back to our cabins, the thought that struck me was, *"Lady Justice never takes a vacation, and apparently, neither would we."*

In cabin #331, Luke and Gwen Larson looked in dismay at the room cards they had taken from room #415.

"Albert and Martha Wallace! Who are these people?" Luke asked. "How could this have happened?"

"Louis hacked into the ship's log and assured us that the Stewarts would be in #415. He must have made a mistake," Gwen replied, "or --- maybe they changed rooms at the last minute. Louis doesn't make mistakes like that."

"Regardless of how it happened," Luke replied, "we've got a real problem. The ship's security has to know by now and they will be on full alert. They're going to have people roaming the halls every night. We can't take the chance of hitting them in their room again. We have stops at Ketchikan and Juneau before we reach Skagway. Maybe we can get to them on their shore excursions."

"We can't even call Louis until we reach Ketchikan. There's no cell service this far from shore."

"Well, as soon as we hit port, Louis needs to hack into the system again to find out what they've booked for shore excursions. He probably didn't do that earlier. They were supposed to be dead by now."

"By the time we reach Skagway," Luke said, "they will be!"

CHAPTER 7

Day #2-Ketchikan, Alaska

At 6:00 A.M., Luke Larson was sitting on the side of his bunk with his cell phone in his hands.

"Come on, damn it! Bars! I need bars!"

"Cussing at it won't give you service any quicker," Gwen said. "Chill out! We have to be patient and stay calm. Louis will know what to do."

"Maybe so, but cussing makes me feel better. At least I'm doing something. Yes! I have bars!"

Quickly he dialed the familiar number and Louis French answered. "Is it done?"

"No, it is not done," Luke replied. "We took care of the occupants of cabin #415 and disposed of their bodies without a hitch, but then we discovered that it was not the Stewarts --- it was a couple by the name of Albert and Martha Wallace."

"Impossible!" French replied. "I confirmed their room myself. Hang on."

Luke could hear the tapping of computer keys.

French came back on the line, "Son-of-a-bitch! They were upgraded to a balcony suite at the last minute, #169. You will try again tonight, yes?"

"No, I don't think that's wise. Security people were all over the ship last night. We've lost the element of surprise. We thought maybe while they were ashore --- on an excursion. Can you look up their itinerary?"

"Hang on," more tapping. "Yes, I have it. I doubt you will have much opportunity today. Your stay in Ketchikan is very brief --- you must be back on board by two-thirty this afternoon and the Stewarts will be on a bus tour most of that time. Your best bet will be in Juneau. I will email the remainder of their shore excursions to you. If you need my assistance, I can get away from the University for a few hours. Keep me informed."

"We will," Luke replied. "One way or the other, the Stewarts will be dead before we reach Skagway!"

By the time I pried my eyes open the next morning, we had docked in our first port of call, Ketchikan. *

I looked out of our window and to my dismay, the sky was bleak and a steady rain was falling.

The clock said 7:30 and we were to board for our first excursion at 9:00. I shook Maggie awake and we quickly showered and dressed.

By prior arrangement, the four of us met the Stewarts at the Lido buffet for breakfast at 8:00.

* See photo, page 216

I was relieved when we stepped off of the elevator and Mark and Amy were waiting for us.

"Since you're here, I trust there were no incidents last night," I said.

"We didn't sleep much, but there were no incidents," Mark replied. "We threw the extra lock and put the chair under the door handle just as you suggested. I felt like we were in a Boston Blackie movie."

I was surprised that a guy Mark's age had even heard of Boston Blackie.

Fortunately, we had all booked the same excursion, a bus tour of the Ketchikan Highlights and a trip to the Totem Bight State Park.

After a quick breakfast, we returned to our cabins to gather our gear for the day ashore.

We were about to head out to meet our friends when my cell phone rang. Cell coverage had been practically non-existent since we left Vancouver and I had nearly forgotten about the phone.

"Hello, Walt here."

"Hi Walt, this is your dad. How's it going? Everything okay there?"

"Sure, Dad. Everything's fine. We're having a great time."

I saw no reason to tell the old man that two people had been murdered six doors down from our cabin.

"Well, I don't want to put a damper on your trip, but something's come up that I think you should know about."

That didn't sound good. "Okay, what's going on?"

"Here, I'll let Willie tell you."

I heard him handing the phone to my old friend.

"Mr. Walt, didn' mean to mess up yo' trip, but I hear'd something' from Louie de Lip dat I thought you ought to know."

"Spit it out, Willie."

"Louie sez dat Benny Bondell is in town."

"So? Who is Benny Bondell?" Then the name rang a bell. "That wouldn't be Mario Bondell's brother would it?"

"Yes, Mr. Walt, it would, an' Louie sez dat Benny is lookin' to even de score wit' the woman what kilt his brudder."

That woman was my friend, Mary Murphy.

Mario Bondell had broken into the Three Trails twice while Mary was away and taken the rent money the tenants had left in her apartment. On the night in question, Mary had left her apartment but returned early because she was coming down with a cold. Bondell was unaware that she had returned. When he broke into her apartment, he found Mary quietly listening to Johnny Mathis records. He pulled a switchblade, threatened Mary and pocketed another handful of rent envelopes. Mary was prepared this time. She pulled a revolver that one of the tenants had loaned her and followed Bondell out the door. She ordered him to stop and when he did, he held up the switchblade and threatened to return and finish the job. Mary, fearing for her life, pulled the trigger, and that was the end of Mario Bondell. Mary was charged with second-degree murder but was found innocent due to the good work of defense attorney, Suzanne Romero. Now, it appeared that Mario's brother was in town to avenge his brother's death.

"Does Mary know about this?" I asked.

"Yeah, I tod 'er. She's half mad an' half skeered. She said if the guy come around she'd whack him too, but I could see dat she was skeered."

"Thanks, Willie. Let me talk to Dad again."

Dad came back on the line, "Any ideas, Sonny?"

"Well, it sounds like I'd better come home. How can I enjoy a vacation when I know there is a killer stalking one of my best friends?"

"Where are you, Son?"

"Ketchikan."

"Then you have a problem," Dad replied. "The only International flights are out of Anchorage and you probably can't get a charter to Anchorage until you get to Juneau. It would be at least two days until you got back home and by then it might be too late. Let us handle things here. What you need to do is call your captain. Let him know what's going on. Maybe he can assign a patrol car to the hotel."

I felt helpless. I knew that Dad was right. "Okay, I'll call the captain. Maybe you and Willie can stay with Mary at the hotel, or better yet, bring her to our building. She can stay in our apartment. You have a key."

"Sure thing," Dad replied. "You make your call and we'll take care of things here --- and don't worry --- just enjoy your trip. We'll keep in touch."

"*Yeah, right*," I thought as I clicked off the phone. Two people had been murdered, our new friends were in danger and a killer bent on revenge was stalking my friend back home. It seemed that our relaxing Alaskan cruise was going to hell in a hand basket!

John Williams hung up the phone. "Looks like it's up to us, Willie. Walt's counting on us."

"So wot's de plan?" Willie asked.

"Looks like we have two choices," John replied. "We can bring Mary over here and try to hide her and hope the guy gives up and goes away --- or--- we can catch the son-of-a-bitch and make sure he goes away."

"I'se kinda partial to dat last one," Willie said with a grin, "but how we gonna do it?"

"I have an idea," he replied, "but it's going to take some finagling."

"Den let's finagle!" Willie said.

"You wait here until I get back. I'm going over to the Senior Center to see if I can get Annie to help us."

"Who's dis Annie person?" Willie asked. "Don't 'member you talkin' 'bout her befo'."

"You'll see," John said, smiling.

John parked at the Senior Center and went directly to the office of the administrator, Leo Manley. "Hey, Leo, how's it hanging?"

"John, what are you doing here today?"

"I need a favor, Leo. You know that my son, Walt, owns the Three Trails Hotel."

Leo nodded.

"Well, there's twenty single guys living there --- some of them getting up in years and I'm worried that they just aren't prepared for an emergency. Bernice and I learned so much from your CPR class, I was wondering if we might borrow Resusci Annie for an evening to give them some training?"

"John, you're not a qualified instructor."

"No, but Walt's been through all the training at the Police Academy. He's going to teach the class --- oh, and he'll have another of his cop buddies there to help him."

John figured that if he was going to tell a fib, he might as well tell a big one.

Leo thought about it. "I suppose if two police officers are in charge it would be okay --- but --- two things."

"Sure, anything," John said eagerly.

"I have to have Annie back by the day after tomorrow. We have another class then."

"No problem. What else?"

"Guard Annie with your life. She cost us

$8,000 and we can't afford another one."

"Absolutely!" John swallowed hard. He hoped that he could keep that promise.

John placed the life-sized mannequin in the front passenger seat and fastened the seatbelt securely around her.

Annie's face was copied from the death mask of an unidentified young woman reputedly drowned in the Seine River around the late 1880's. She wasn't exactly the picture of the girl next door.

As John drove from the Senior Center to his apartment building, he couldn't help but notice the craning necks and astonished expressions from the drivers of the passing cars.

When John pulled up in front of the apartment building, Willie and Jerry were waiting on the front porch.

John waved them to the car and rolled down the window, "Guys, meet Annie."

"Wot de hell you doin' wit a blow up doll?" Willie asked. "I thought you had Bernice fo' dat kind o' stuff."

"She's not *THAT* kind of doll, Willie. She's designed to help train people in emergency procedures like CPR."

"So how's dis doll gonna help ketch dat Bondell creep?"

"Get in and I'll show you."

Willie and Jerry piled into the back seat and the four of them headed to the Three Trails Hotel.

At 8:45, the six of us boarded a bus that was to take us on a tour of Ketchikan and to the Totem Bight State Park.

The rain had been falling steadily all morning and passengers boarding the bus were irritating those already seated by shaking the excess water from their umbrellas and poking them with their tips as they passed by.

Our tour guide was quick to point out that this was a normal day in Ketchikan, which was known as the wettest city in Alaska and in much of North America for that matter, with an annual rainfall of over twelve feet. It seemed to us that a foot of that fell during our brief stay in the city.

Ketchikan, being the southernmost city in Alaska was one of the first stopping points for the prospectors heading to the gold fields.

In the late 1890's a booming business of saloons and brothels grew to satisfy the carnal needs of the gold-hungry travelers. At one time, it was reported that there were more than fifty establishments where travel-weary miners could get some TLC.

As the bus passed over a bridge, the tour guide pointed to a path leading down to the famous Creek Street where most of the bawdy houses had been located. "That's the 'Married Man's Trail'," she said. "The men living up here on the hill would take this path down to Creek Street when they wanted to engage in some extracurricular activity."

An old man in his eighties a few seats in front of us blurted out, "Guess I'd better head down to Creek Street when we get back. Been looking for some 'extracurricular activity'."

His wife, sitting next to him, punched him in the arm, "Shut up Earl. You wouldn't know what to do with it if you had it."

That evoked a round of snickers from the passengers. Probably not the response Earl had hoped for.

"Sorry, sir," the guide said, "prostitution was outlawed in 1953, but I'm sure you could find a nice T-shirt."

After the city tour, we headed to Totem Bight State Park where we visited a Tlingit Indian clan house and saw totem poles carved by the Raven and Eagle clans. Each pole told a story with its intricate and sometimes grotesque carvings.

As I stared at one pole, there was something familiar about it but I couldn't quite put my finger on it --- then it occurred to me --- one carving in the pole looked exactly like Old Man Feeney, sitting on the can in bathroom #3 at the Three Trails! I made a mental note to ask him if by any chance he was part Tlingit. After further reflection, I thought better of the idea. It just wasn't worth the hassle. *

---

* See photo, page 217

After the bus tour, we shopped the establishments along Creek Street, which in many ways was like Front Street on Maui. Souvenir shops, restaurants and jewelry stores lined the famous street. We heard from another passenger that there were over fifty jewelry stores in Ketchikan. I suppose that the fifty jewelry stores took the place of the fifty brothels that once drew travelers from afar. The thing that they had in common was that you could get screwed in either one.

We all did the tourist thing, buying T-shirts and other worthless crap for our friends back home. After a relaxing lunch of fish and chips we headed back to the ship.

We set sail at precisely three o'clock, but I missed the departure. I was zonked out in our cabin.

Maggie woke me just in time to get showered and changed before we met our friends in the Rotterdam Dining Room.

We had decided that Mark and Amy would join us as the extra couple at the six-seater table. We did this for two reasons --- so that we could keep an eye on them and to avoid having to spend another grueling evening with Paul and Irene.

I had to give Den credit. He quite correctly observed that Ox and I were struggling with the fare offered by the featured chefs on the cruise, so he whispered quietly that he could probably come up with some New York Strip steaks and a baked potato. The guy saved our lives. While our wives were enjoying the Roasted Rack of Lamb with Smoked-

Paprika Crust, we were gnawing on big chunks of real beef and a potato slathered in butter.

I noticed Paul and Irene sitting at the table next to us. Her mouth was going non-stop and she didn't even pause when she gave me a little finger wave. The entrees hadn't yet been delivered, but I could see that her table companions already had that Irene-induced zombie stare. I was willing to bet that they'd be eating elsewhere tomorrow night.

After the meal, we went to the ship's theatre where we thoroughly enjoyed a Broadway-style production of singing and dance.

In spite of the rain, it had been a good day.

Although I couldn't stop worrying about the creep stalking Mary, no one had tried to kill our new friends and we had loved our tour of Ketchikan.

Maybe we were making too much of this 'killing for gold' theory and the poor folks in cabin #415 were really the targets in the first place.

As I crawled into bed, I tried to put all of the bad stuff out of my mind. Here I was, on a fabulous ship, with the love of my life, in one of the most beautiful places on earth.

Maggie crawled into bed and snuggled up beside me.

With the warmth of her body and the gentle rocking of the ship, I was soon asleep.

Luke and Gwen Larson had been shadowing the Stewarts all day. They had hoped to catch them alone in some deserted place, but four other passengers seemed to be stuck to them like glue.

When the six of them boarded the ship in the afternoon, Gwen followed them to their cabins and returned to report their room numbers to Luke.

"The big guy and his woman are in #399 and the old couple are in #401."

Luke punched the familiar number and waited.

"Louis here. What do you have to report?"

"We've been shadowing the Stewarts all day and they seem to have picked up some friends --- they've been inseparable. We thought maybe you should check them out --- cabin #'s 399 and 401."

Luke heard tapping in the computer, then, "Shit!" and more tapping.

Louis French came back on the line. "We may have a complication. George and Judy Wilson are in #399 and they're both cops. Walter and Maggie Williams are in #401 and Walter is a cop. I think we have to assume that the Stewarts found out about the murders in their old cabin, got freaked out and made contact with these people. They're all from Kansas City."

"So what should we do?" Luke asked. "Gwen and I are no match for three cops."

"Then I must join you," French replied. "You'll be in Juneau tomorrow. I will take a day of leave from the University. Together, we'll find a way to make this work. All we need is the right opportunity. Try to secure an extra seat for me on the shore excursions."

"Maybe we should just pack it in," Luke offered. "We had our best chance and we blew it."

"Nonsense," French replied. "There's a stash of gold buried somewhere in Skagway, and by God, we're going to get it!"

John parked his car a block away from the Three Trails and watched the black and white that sat idling in front of the hotel.

"Ain't nobody gonna come wit dat cop sittin' dere," Willie said.

"Just be patient and watch," John replied.

About a half hour later, the car's lights flashed on, the siren blared and the cop pulled out into traffic.

"See," John said, "the guy was there as long as there was nothing more urgent happening, but he was obviously called away. Who's watching the store now?"

"Us and maybe that Bondell guy," Jerry replied.

"Exactly!" John said. "Time for us to get to work."

The three of them carried Annie to Mary's front door and knocked.

Mary opened the door just a crack. "What are you guys doing here and what the hell is that?" she asked, seeing the mannequin between the three guys. "You ain't got nothing kinky in mind, I hope."

"No, nothing kinky," John said. "Now let us in before someone sees us."

She opened the door and they all piled inside.

"You still ain't told me what you're doing here."

"We're going to get this Bondell guy out of your hair for good," John replied, "and Annie's going to help us."

"I hope this ugly bitch has a gun, cause I don't have one no more. The cops took it."

"Not going to need a gun," John replied. "We're going to capture him with our wits."

"Then I hope they're a lot sharper than I think they are or you're gonna get us all killed!"

"Oh, ye of little faith," John said. "Just help me get the room set up."

They moved the TV set to the opposite end of the room so that it faced the door and placed Mary's lounge chair in front of it.

They sat Annie in the chair, but her head was below the headrest.

"Nope, this won't work," John said. "Phone books! Do you have any phone books?"

"Lots of 'em," Mary said, heading for a closet.

Three phone books later, the back of Annie's head could be clearly seen above the chair and she appeared to be watching the TV.

"Now comes the tricky part," John said. "Listen very carefully if you want to come out of this in one piece. The guy is going to sneak in and put a round or two in Annie. That's when we come in. We will each be hiding behind something heavy, and one by one, we will draw his fire until his gun is empty. That's when we'll nab him."

"Uhhh, draw his fire?" Jerry asked. "You mean we're going to make the guy shoot at us?"

"That's the plan," John said. "The trick is to duck --- really fast!"

"Duck!" Jerry said. "That reminds me of a joke. How do you get down off a duck?"

He didn't wait for a response. "You don't! You get down off of an elephant!"

"Jesus, Jerry! Can't you ever be serious?"

"Are you kidding? If I was being serious, I'd be scared to death!"

"Nothing to be scared of. Just yell at the guy and then duck. I'll go first, Willie second and Jerry third. When he's out of ammo, we'll have one more little surprise for him."

The room was pitch black except for the light from the TV where Jay Leno was entertaining the audience with his monologue.

Benny Bondell peered through the window and saw the silhouette of the head of the woman that had killed his brother. It was payback time.

He slipped his lock pick in the door and heard the 'click' as it popped open. He turned the knob and pushed. There was a low 'creeeeek' as the old door opened on its rusty hinges, but the laughter from the TV covered the noise.

He slipped into the room, drew his pistol and fired two quick rounds into the back of the old woman's head. He saw the head explode and knew that he had hit pay dirt.

From somewhere to his right, a voice filled the room, "Is that all you've got, creep?"

Bondell turned and fired in the direction of the voice.

From the other side of the room came another voice, "Yo mama is an ugly ho!"

He swung around and fired again.

From the far end of the room, behind the TV, another, somewhat softer voice was heard, "A horse walks into a bar."

Bondell fired two shots into Jay Leno and the TV screen exploded into a million pieces.

From his right side, the first voice spoke again, "How many bullets you got left, creep?"

Bondell turned and pulled the trigger, but all he got was a 'click'. Seeing that his gun was empty and that he was obviously outnumbered, he turned to run.

"**NOW**!" John shouted.

He and Willie pulled the wire that had been lying on the floor between them catching the foot of the fleeing Bondell.

As soon as he hit the floor, the overhead light came on and he found himself staring at a mountain of a woman standing over him with a baseball bat."

"Got any more brothers? If you do, send them around and we'll take care of them too!"

One whack and Bondell was out for the count.

John dialed 911 and soon sirens could be heard in the distance.

John grimaced as he surveyed the decapitated Resusci Annie. "Leo's not going to be happy about this! Anybody got an extra eight grand laying around?"

Mary looked at her shattered TV. "Been wanting to get me a new TV anyway. One of them flat screen things."

Jerry rose up from behind the TV, "I didn't get to finish my joke. A horse walks into a bar and the bartender says, 'Hey buddy, why the long face?'"

Willie said, "You all a bunch o' damn fools --

- but we did good, din' we?"

Mary grabbed him and gave him a big bear hug. "Yes, Willie, we did good!"

CHAPTER 8

Day #2-Juneau, Alaska

When my eyes popped open, the first thing I did was peek out of the window. After a full day in rainy Ketchikan, I was afraid that with a second one I might start to mildew.

To my great relief, the first rays of the sun were peeking over the snow-capped mountain range. It looked like it was going to be a beautiful day.

We weren't scheduled to dock in Juneau until ten o'clock, so Maggie and Judy talked us into breakfast in the fancy Rotterdam.

We hooked up with Mark and Amy and watched the glorious Alaskan scenery pass by as waiters in starched coats served us the exact same stuff that we had been getting for ourselves in the Lido Buffet --- but the girls were happy --- and as every guy knows, if the girls ain't happy, nobody's happy!

The six of us were scheduled to board the busses for our shore excursion just minutes after the ship docked, so we scurried back to our cabins to prepare for the day's adventure.

When we entered, the cell phone was buzzing.

I read the message, "New text."

I scrolled down and saw a very brief message from Captain Short, "Benny Bondell behind bars. Have a great trip."

I was about to relay the message to Maggie when the phone rang.

"Walt, here."

"Hi, Sonny," I just wanted to let you know that Benny Bondell is out of the picture so you can quit worrying about Mary. She's fine."

"How? --- What happened? How did it go down?"

"Long story, Walt. Don't want to bore you. I know you've got lots to do. We'll talk when you get back."

I could tell that he was stonewalling me.

"Dad, I want to know ---."

He cut me off. "All you need to know right now is that everything here is just hunky-dory. We're all fine. Now go have some fun!"

I heard the 'click'. He had hung up.

I was definitely relieved that Bondell was no longer a threat to Mary, but now my curiosity was aroused. I was almost anxious to get home so that I could hear how Bondell was captured and by whom. Like Dad said, it was probably a long story and I was willing to bet that it was a doozy.

As soon as the ship was docked, the six of us were herded, along with fifty other passengers, to another bus.

The whole process of de-boarding and being directed to our busses reminded me of the old TV show, *Rawhide*.

I could see the young Clint Eastwood as the cattle drive's ramrod, Rowdy Yates, herding the cows along as Frankie Laine sang the theme song, *"Move 'em out, head 'em up, head 'em up, move 'em on. Move 'em out, head 'em up: Rawhide!"*

I figured it was all part of the experience. If you don't want to be herded --- don't go on a cruise!

Luke and Gwen Larson met Louis French in the parking lot where the busses were idling.

"Sorry, Louis, but the excursion was sold out. We couldn't get you a ticket."

"Probably just as well," he replied, looking at the long line trying to board the bus. "With all of these people, our opportunities would probably be limited. Just keep an eye on them and give me a call when your tour is finished. The ship doesn't leave port until ten-thirty tonight. We'll get our chance."

The Larson's nodded and fell in line behind the Stewarts.

The first stop of our tour was the Macaulay Salmon Hatchery.

I wasn't exactly trembling with excitement over this stop. Maggie and I had been to the trout hatchery on Table Rock Lake in Branson, Missouri, and I figured that if you've seen one hatchery, you've seen them all.

A perky young guide who led us through the facility that was perched over the beautiful Sheep Creek met us.

As we looked down into the swirling waters below, I could see huge salmon, weighing between five and ten pounds swimming upriver against the strong current.

Our guide explained that most of these salmon had been reared at the facility and released, to spend anywhere from two to five years roaming the Pacific Ocean.

At the appropriate time, when some magic thing in their DNA went off, they would return to exactly the same mountain stream where they had hatched, to spawn.

After a harrowing trip up river against the current, battling bears, sea lions, seals, killer whales and, of course, man, the brave fish would spawn and then die. If these were humans instead of fish, their story would have made a fantastic romance novel.

Next, we were off to the Mendenhall Glacier.

It was a beautiful twelve-mile ride from Juneau to the glacier. We parked alongside at least two-dozen other busses. I later learned that a half million people visit the famous glacier each year. It looked like most of them were there that day.

A fantastic visitor's center was perched high above Mendenhall Lake, and on the far side of the lake, the massive 12 mile long glacier glimmered in the sun. Chunks of ice that had calved off of the glacier floated in the frigid water. *

After touring the visitor center and snapping dozens of photos of the big ice cube, Mark and Amy wanted to take one of the half-dozen hikes that ran from the parking lot into the wilderness.

The different trails took varying times to complete, from a half hour up to five hours. The Stewarts were disappointed to learn that the bus schedule would only allow for a half hour hike on the Trail of Time.

As they headed off into the forest, Ox tapped me on the shoulder, "Shouldn't one of us go with them?"

"Do you really think that someone would try something here?" I asked. "There must be a bazillion people running around the place."

"Yeah, but how many of them are out in the woods?"

I had seen one other couple follow the Stewarts as they disappeared down the trail.

"You know, you're right," I said. "If someone's really after them for that gold, we can't let our guard down. One of us should go."

"I'll flip you for it," Ox said.

---

* See photo, page 217

He pulled a quarter out of his pocket and flipped it in the air. "Call it."

"Heads," naturally, it was tails.

Now I am fully aware that the statistical probability of a coin coming up heads is 50%, but somehow, I have been able to defy the laws of probability all of my life.

It makes no difference whether it's a coin flip or anything else that has only two possible outcomes --- whichever one I choose, it's always the opposite.

Any time that I try to plug in one of those electric cords that have one prong bigger than the other, there should be an even chance that I will get it right half the time --- but it never happens.

One profession that I will absolutely NEVER consider is being on the bomb squad. I've seen the movies where the guy has ten seconds to decide whether to cut the red wire or the blue one before everyone is blown to hell. No matter which one I would choose, it would be the wrong one.

Ox knows this and has used that knowledge multiple times in our three years of working together. That particular moment was no exception.

"Oh gee, Walt," he said with a big grin, "tails! Imagine that. Have a nice hike."

"Fine! When you find the girls, please tell Maggie where I am and that you've screwed me again."

"Well, I'll tell them the first part," he said with a wave as he ambled to the concession stand.

I headed down the path where I had seen the

Stewarts enter the woods and the first thing I encountered were signs warning hikers to beware of bears.

"Just great," I thought. *"The one person that might actually have a chance against a bear is probably wolfing down a chili dog about now."*

The path was quite curvy and wooden bridges spanned bog-like terrain and swiftly running streams. I could only see a few yards ahead of me due to all of the twists and turns.

As I rounded a corner at the end of a particularly long open stretch, I saw Mark and Amy. They seemed to be fascinated by something in the trees just off the path.

The couple that I had seen follow them in were right behind them and seemed to be advancing toward them at an unusually rapid pace.

I knew that there was no way that I could catch up to them quickly, so I cupped my hands and shouted, "MARK! AMY! WAIT UP!"

They turned when they heard my voice and I noticed that the other couple slowed their pace.

When I finally caught up, I heard bits of conversation. "Mark and Amy Stewart from Kansas City."

"We're the Larson's from Washington State. Seen any bears?"

"No, just that old guy," Mark said pointing to a porcupine perched on a tree limb about ten feet off the trail."

When I came huffing up, Mark said, "This is

Walt. He's --- uhhh --- a friend of ours."

"Nice to meet you," the man said, extending his hand. "Luke Larson and this is my wife, Gwen."

As I shook the man's hand, I felt ridiculous thinking that this young couple could have been a danger to the Stewarts. I figured that I was getting a bit paranoid.

We finished the hike without encountering either bears or muggers.

The bus was nearly full by the time we emerged from the woods.

As I walked past Ox, he couldn't help but give me a hard time. "How was your hike? Beautiful, I'll bet."

"Shut up and wipe the chili off your chin."

Our last stop was the Gold Creek Alaskan Salmon Bake.

The camp was located just off of the highway, far back into the forest along the bank of Salmon Creek.

When we climbed off of the bus, the mixture of aromas that filled the air made my mouth water.

Huge slabs of wild-caught salmon were roasting on a grill over an open Alder-wood fire. *

A buffet had been set up with baked beans, rice, cornbread and other tasty stuff. We got plates, made our selections from the buffet and headed to the grill.

---

* See photo, page 218

A crusty old guy transferred the salmon steaks from the fire to our plates and asked if we wanted sauce.

I looked at the pan of brown gooey stuff bubbling in an old brown pot. "What kind of sauce?"

"Brown sugar."

I figured that it couldn't be too bad.

We took our places at long picnic tables. The first bite of the salmon hit my mouth and Ox's at the same time. I could tell by the expression on his face that we had just experienced a culinary miracle.

All either of could say was, "Ohhhhh! Ohhhh!"

I had never tasted anything quite like it in my life.

We went back for seconds and were still gobbling the sweet fish long after the rest of our party was finished.

There was plenty to explore around the old gold camp. Pans were provided for the hardy folks that wanted to brave the icy water to pan for gold and marshmallows were available to be roasted over an open fire.

I had kept one eye on Mark and Amy while my other eye was on my salmon. They had wandered around the camp, roasted a few marshmallows and had just headed up a wooded trail that ran alongside Salmon Creek.

I wasn't too concerned until I saw the couple that had followed them on the glacier trail fall in behind them.

Coincidence? Maybe --- maybe not!

"Watch my plate," I said to Ox. "Don't let anyone take it. I'm not through yet."

"Somethin' wrong?" Ox mumbled with a mouthful of salmon.

"Probably not. Just making sure."

The path followed the curves of Salmon Creek and it was easy to spot the big fish fighting their way upstream to spawn and die.

I rounded a bend, and a hundred yards ahead I saw Mark and Amy staring into a gigantic hole in the side of the mountain. It was probably the entrance to the old mine that had been abandoned years ago. *

The only other people on the trail were Luke and Gwen and they were going to be at the mine opening long before I would.

I was faced with a dilemma --- yell out again and have them think that I'm a damned old fool or do nothing and hope that they do the same.

It didn't take me long to decide. Better to look foolish than to look back at the moment with regret.

"HEY, PROSPECTORS! WAIT FOR ME!"

Luke and Gwen had reached the Stewarts just as I shouted. All four of them turned to face me.

A big smile broke out on two of the faces. Not so much on the other two.

"Well, here we are again," Luke said, forcing a smile. "We're going to have to quit meeting like this. People will talk."

---

* See photo, page 219

"I'm glad you showed up, Walt," Amy said. "Mark wanted to explore in this old mine, but I don't think it's safe. Maybe you can talk some sense into him."

I looked at the entrance that had yellow tape across it and a sign that said, "DANGER - NO ADMITTANCE."

I was just about to weigh in as a party pooper when we heard the bus honking its horn in the distance.

"I guess that settles it," Amy said, taking Mark's hand. "We have to go or we'll miss the bus."

We all headed back down the trail, but something told me that not everyone was happy that I showed up again.

It was about three in the afternoon when the bus dropped us off in the parking lot by the wharf where the cruise ship was docked.

Since the ship wouldn't sail until ten-thirty that night, we still had lots of time to see the sights of Juneau.

One of the attractions that had caught our eye when the ship had first docked was the Mount Roberts Tramway just a short walk from the wharf.

One of the things that I had noticed about the Alaskan coastal cities was that they all seemed to be built on whatever land happened to be available between the sea on one side and the mountains on the other. Juneau was a perfect example. The base of Mount Roberts, right in the heart of Juneau, rose almost straight up to over 4,000 feet to the summit.

The Tramway consisted of two opposing gondolas traveling 1,800 feet, almost straight up, on huge cables from sea level to a restaurant, theatre and nature center perched on the side of the mountain. *

It had been billed as one of Alaska's best attractions. After we purchased our tickets and were directed to the loading area, I discovered why. Counting the Statendam, there were a total of six cruise ships docked at the Juneau wharf and it looked like every passenger from all six ships had decided to take the tram at the same time. The line snaked around endless barriers as the travelers waited for the gondolas to make their round trip to the top and back.

We fell in line behind a woman that obviously had a seeing impairment. She held a red-tipped cane in one hand and the leash to a big black lab in the other. I had to admire the woman's spunk. Navigating the crowded tourist attraction was a struggle for me even with all of my faculties. I could only imagine what it was like for her.

---

* See photo, page 219

Judy, being a dog lover, asked the woman if she could pet the lab. The woman politely said, "no" since the dog was 'working', and that was that.

The big dog seemed oblivious to the hundreds of people that crowded around him --- except for me. He raised his big head, looked me in the eye and buried his wet nose in my crotch.

"Looks like you have an admirer," Ox said with a grin.

I am at a total loss as to why, during my pathetic life, there have been WAY more dogs acquainted with my crotch than women --- not a statistic that I'm proud of.

At last it was our turn to board the gondola. The thing was supposed to hold sixty passengers and by the time the door closed, I knew how a sardine must feel. Thank goodness the trip to the top only lasted six minutes.

We had only gone a few hundred feet when I felt a gentle probing of my rear end. I guessed, incorrectly, that Maggie was taking the opportunity to demonstrate her attraction to her mate.

I reached around, expecting to find the hand of my sweetie, but instead grabbed hold of a wet nose. Apparently the big lab had decided to check out my backside.

The wait in line had been grueling and the ride to the top had been claustrophobic, but when we stepped out of the gondola onto the observation deck, it was quite obvious that the view was worth the hassle.

Almost directly below was the city of Juneau and we could see for miles in every direction, from the Gastineau Channel on the south to the Chilkat Mountains on the north and to Douglas Island across the Channel. Spectacular! *

We were a bit dry and exhausted from the ordeal, so our first stop was the Timberline Bar and Grill where we all enjoyed a refreshing beverage while drinking in the marvelous view.

A young lady came through the restaurant announcing that the next presentation in the theatre would be starting in a few minutes. It was an eighteen-minute film about the culture of the Tlingit Indians of Southeast Alaska. We decided to attend.

It was just after four o'clock when we exited the theatre. We still had an hour and a half to kill before we were to re-board for our next fine dining experience at the Rotterdam.

There were several trails leading from the lodge up onto the mountainside and our young charges were eager to explore a bit more of the Alaskan wilderness.

We found out from a guide that the most popular trail was the Alpine Loop Trail, which, as the name implied, made a half-mile loop up the steep mountain and back to the lodge. It was the shortest trail and would take maybe forty-five minutes depending on how much time was spent gawking.

---

* See photo, page 220

We were about to head out when Ox held up his hand, "If I'm going to be out there forty-five minutes and exerting, I need to make a potty stop."

"Me, too," Judy said. "You guys go on and we'll catch up."

We were just heading out the door when a middle-aged fellow tapped me on the arm. "Excuse me. I don't mean to be a bother, but I'm by myself and I wonder if you'd mind taking a photo of me on the observation platform with the Channel in the background?"

I was about to beg off when Amy said, "Go ahead, Walt. We'll be fine. You can catch up when Ox and Judy are out of the restroom."

I looked around and seeing no one in particular, and specifically not the couple that had showed up on our last two stops, I reluctantly agreed.

"I really appreciate this," the man said as he posed on the platform. "My kids back in California have been bugging me to send pictures, but it's hard to do when you're alone. I'm Louis French, by the way."

"Walt and Maggie Williams," I said, snapping the picture. "I gather you're not used to traveling alone."

"Not really," he replied. "My wife passed away six months ago and this is my first time out."

I felt like an idiot. "Sorry to hear that," I said, sheepishly.

"It happens," he said with a sigh. "Part of life, I guess. Anyway, thank you very much."

French headed to the line of people waiting for the next gondola down the mountain just as Ox and Judy came around the corner.

"How come you guys aren't on the trail, and where are Mark and Amy?" Ox asked.

I pointed to French standing in line, "That guy asked us to snap his picture. The Stewarts went on ahead. I made sure no one was following them, but we need to hurry to catch up."

The first part of the trail was relatively easy, but then the climb became steeper and Ox was soon huffing and puffing. Most of the trail was fairly wide, but in some places, it was only three feet wide with the mountain rising on one side and a sheer drop-off on the other.

Signs along the trail bore the same warning as the tattoo purported to be on the inside of a hooker's thigh, "Slippery when wet!"

We came to a wide spot with a spectacular view and Ox held up his hand. "Rest stop!"

I had tried to keep my own gasping to a minimum and I wasn't about to argue.

We had just plopped down when from up ahead we heard a blood-curdling scream.

"EEEEEEAAAAAAAHHHH!"

We were all on our feet in an instant, double-timing up the trail.

The first "HELP" was faint, but as we climbed, it became louder. "HELP!" HELP!"

We came to a sharp bend in the trail and when

we looked over the edge, we were horrified to see Mark perched on a rock outcropping twenty feet below us.

Amy was just ten feet below the trail, but her predicament was much more serious --- she was hanging onto the base of a cedar tree and her feet were dangling loose. If she lost her grip, she would plummet hundreds of feet to the rocks below.

"We need a rope," Ox said. "We have to go back to the lodge for a rope!"

We could see the terror in Amy's eyes, "I --- I don't think I can hold on much longer. Help me!"

"It would take at least fifteen minutes to get back to the lodge and another fifteen back up here. She'll never hold on that long," Judy said.

I had a thought, but the idea absolutely petrified me. I have two phobias, spiders and heights. Looking over the edge to the jagged rocks hundreds of feet below gave me the willys, but I couldn't think of a better option.

"Ox, do you think you can support my weight?"

"They don't call me 'Ox' for nothing," he replied.

"Then here's what we have to do --- you'll grab my feet and lower me over the ledge. Amy and I will lock hands and you can pull us both up. Think you can handle it?"

"Walt!" Maggie shrieked. "Surely you're not thinking of going over that edge!"

"I'm certainly open to any other suggestions,"

I replied.

She had none.

"I can do it," Ox said, "but we'd better hurry."

"Okay," I said with more confidence than I was feeling, "get on your knees and grab my ankles. I'll ease myself over the edge and you can slowly lower me down. You may have to lie on your stomach to get me low enough to reach her. When Ox is on his stomach, you girls each sit on one of his legs to keep him stable. Are we ready?"

"Let's do it!" he said.

I got on my belly and eased my chest out over the side of the cliff. I felt Ox's big paws around my ankle. It wasn't too bad until the moment that I had to completely slide off and dangle upside down relying totally on the strength of my friend.

I closed my eyes and slid out into the void. I felt the blood rushing to my head and hoped that I wouldn't pass out.

"*Don't look down. Don't look down.*" I kept saying to myself, but I knew that eventually, I would have to open my eyes.

When I did peek out, I saw Amy a good two feet below my outstretched arms.

"More! I need more!" I yelled.

"That's all I've got unless I bend out over the cliff myself --- but then I've lost all my leverage --- the only thing that would be holding me is the girls."

"I --- I can't hold on much longer!" Amy wailed.

"We can do it," Judy said. "Go slow --- but GO!"

I felt Ox shifting his weight forward and when the big man's stomach was over the edge, he leaned down giving me just enough to reach the tree Amy was clutching.

"Okay, Amy," I said, trying to be reassuring, "you need to lock your hand around my wrist and I'll do the same to yours. When we're secure, Ox will lift us up."

"I --- I can't let go," she said as tears rolled down her cheeks. "I'll fall!"

"No you won't. I won't let you!"

"You might want to hurry down there," Ox said. "I'm about to lose my lunch!"

"Amy, look at me!" I said with as much authority as I could muster. "Take my hand --- NOW!"

She looked into my eyes and summoning every ounce of strength that she could muster, she let go of the cedar and lunged for my outstretched hand.

My hand closed around her slender wrist and she grasped mine.

"Now the other one," I said.

She released her grip on the only thing that was firmly anchored to the mountain and we found ourselves dangling in mid-air held only by my partner's grasp.

"Got her!" I said. "Pull us up!"

I felt Ox's muscles tense and we were raised maybe six inches, but we quickly returned to our original position.

"Can't do it!" he said. "I have no leverage hanging out here like this. The girls are going to have to pull me back up to where I can get my elbows on solid ground."

I thought about Maggie weighing a hundred and twenty and Judy weighing a hundred and forty hauling Ox's two hundred and thirty pounds, plus me and Amy, back up the cliff and I got a bad feeling.

"Okay," I heard Judy say, "let's do this together --- one --- two --- three!"

I heard grunting and huffing, but we didn't budge an inch.

"Again!" she said, "one --- two --- three!"

More grunting, but still no movement.

I had never felt so helpless in my life.

My arms were aching and I didn't know how much longer Ox could hold on.

Just when things seemed most desperate, I heard an unfamiliar voice, "HOLY CRAP! WHAT'S GOING ON?"

"We could use a hand here," Judy said.

"Sure! What do you want us to do?"

"Help us pull the big guy back over the lip so we can pull those two up."

I heard some scuffling around, and then slowly we were being lifted.

I heard Ox let out a big sigh and felt myself moving rapidly up the cliff face. When I reached the top, hands reached out and pulled Amy and me onto the trail.

I was breathless and poor Amy was sobbing uncontrollably.

Maggie held me close, "I thought I'd lost you."

"Nope, can't get rid of me that easy," I said with a lot more bravado than I was feeling.

Ox had grabbed the hand of the closest stranger, "Thanks for your help."

"Good thing we decided to take a hike," he said. "I'm Billy and this is my life-partner, Ernie. Glad we could help. Anything else we can do?"

"If you wouldn't mind making the trip back to the lodge, we could sure use a rope," he said pointing to Mark clinging to the ledge below.

"Sure thing, we'll send someone up."

By the time they were out of sight, Amy had regained some of her composure.

"How did this happen?" I asked.

"We were hiking the trail and had just turned this corner when two people came from behind that outcropping and pushed us over the edge."

"Did you see who pushed you?" Ox asked.

"No, it all happened so quickly. One moment we were on the trail and the next moment I was hanging from that tree branch. Do you think --- you know --- the gold?"

"I'd say that was a definite possibility."

The Stewarts were to meet with Alfred Quimby the next day to search for a fortune in gold and it was obvious that someone wanted them out of the way.

CHAPTER 9

Louis French and the Larsons huddled together by the bald eagle exhibit at the nature center where they could see both ends of the Alpine Loop Trail.

A half hour earlier, they had seen two men run to one of the tour guides and have an animated conversation while pointing back up the trail. The tour guide had spoken briefly on her walkie-talkie and shortly afterward, two men with security patches on their shoulders headed up the trail with a coil of rope and a first aid kit.

They suspected that their plan had not been entirely successful.

"You definitely saw them go over the edge of the cliff?" French asked.

"Absolutely!" Luke replied. "The woman screamed bloody murder. We didn't stick around because we didn't want to be seen. We figured that the three cops couldn't be too far behind them."

"I stalled them as long as I could," French said. "I can't imagine how they could have survived that fall."

A few minutes later, they saw the Stewarts, their four friends and the two security guards coming down the trail. The Stewarts had a few cuts and scratches, but seemed to be in pretty good shape considering the fact that they had just been pushed off of a cliff.

When the group was out of sight, Louis said,

"It had to be those damn cops. It doesn't look like we're going to eliminate the Stewarts as long as they're hanging around. I think that we should concentrate on getting rid of those four first and then we'll go after the Stewarts again."

"Any ideas how we can accomplish that?" Gwen asked.

"Yes, I do. You'll get rid of them once and for all tonight. I'll charter a seaplane to Skagway and meet you there tomorrow. Here's what I want you to do ----."

The first thing we all wanted to do after we boarded the ship was to take a long, hot shower. Our bodies ached from the strain and exertion of our experience on the mountainside.

I let Maggie go first while I gulped a handful of ibuprophen and collapsed on the bed.

As I lay there, I replayed the day's events over in my mind.

The Larson's had been right behind the Stewarts all day long, but were nowhere to be seen on Mount Roberts.

Out of the blue, some stranger asks us to take his picture and occupies our attention just long enough for the Stewarts to get a good head start up the mountain where they're attacked by two unseen people --- the Larsons?

I was mulling this over when Maggie stepped out of the shower wrapped in a white fluffy towel.

"Your turn," she announced.

Suddenly, my attention was diverted from the mysterious to the sublime. I pulled my aching body from the bed and was about to reach for the towel when she noticed the look in my eye.

"Back off, Romeo," she said, pulling the towel tighter." In case you hadn't noticed, you're a bit ripe. Get some of that mountain washed off and we'll talk."

She was right, of course, so I turned the water on as hot as I could stand and let the shower beat down on my 70 year old body.

The ibuprophen must have kicked in, and that, along with the steaming shower led me into a state of semi-consciousness. I don't know how long I was in la-la land, but when the water started running ice cold, it was a rude awakening.

As I dried off, I remembered Maggie's words, "Get some of that mountain off and we'll talk."

The mountain was off and I was ready to take her up on her offer, but when I stepped out of the bathroom, Maggie was dressed with her hair combed and make-up on. I had learned a long time ago that when the hair's combed and the make-up's on, it just ain't going to happen.

She must have seen the disappointed look on my face. "Hey, don't blame me! You're the one that zonked out in the shower. We're supposed to meet everyone in the Rotterdam in fifteen minutes, so you'd better hurry."

When the six of us were seated and had given Den our order, Mark spoke, "We had a visitor in our cabin just after we boarded the ship, an Alejandro Reyes, the ship's security officer."

I had wondered how long it would take for Reyes to look for a possible connection between the Stewarts and the murders in cabin #415. They had kept the news of the murders under wraps so far.

"Did he come right out and tell you about the murders?" I asked.

"No, he talked about everything but that. We hadn't cleaned up yet and he asked about our cuts and bruises. We told him that we had a hiking accident. He asked if there had been any problems since we were upgraded to a balcony room, and we told him 'no --- no problems'. We played dumb all the way."

When we were on the mountainside waiting for the rope to arrive to pull Mark up the cliff, we all decided not to tell the security people about the attack. It would only raise questions and there really wasn't anything they could do at that point. Whoever had pushed them was long gone.

"Well, there's no question now that someone knows about the gold," I said. "Tomorrow, we meet Quimby at Skagway. Maybe we can get to the bottom of this once and for all --- until then we all need to be on our toes."

After dinner, we all went to the ship's theatre. A comedian was the featured performer. His witty banter was just the thing that we all needed to take our minds off of nearly being killed.

We had noticed that the vast majority of passengers aboard the Statendam were senior citizens. In fact, Ox had made the comment that he felt like he was on a floating nursing home.

The comedian was obviously quite aware of this fact and much of his monologue was 'old folks' oriented.

"The bartenders have concocted a special drink just for this cruise," he quipped. "It's made of Viagra and prune juice. They call it the 'Get Up and Go'!"

The audience roared and I thought of my old friend, Jerry. He would make a great cruise ship comic.

We were all in a much better mood as we headed back to our cabins.

We had just brushed our teeth and slipped into our jammies when we heard a rhythmic thumping and some thrashing around coming from across the wall in cabin #399.

"Sounds like Ox and Judy might be --- uhhhh --- spawning," Maggie observed.

"Well, there's definitely something 'fishy' going on over there," I replied.

"So are you up for some 'spawning' of your own?" she asked with a flirtatious toss of her head. "As I recall, you were earlier in the evening."

"As long as I don't die right after," I said, slipping my arm around her waist.

"Oh, you won't be dead, but you'll think you've gone to heaven," she said, turning off the light.

After our 'spawn', I wasn't dead, but I was dead tired from the day's adventures and I drifted off into a sound sleep.

I was awakened by Maggie shaking me vigorously, "Walt! Wake up!"

My first thought was that my sweetie had enjoyed our earlier tryst so much, she was back for more. I had taken care of business, if I do say so. "Maggie, maybe in the morning," I mumbled, "I just don't know if I'm up for another one right now."

"No, no, not that. I smell smoke! Wake up!"

That got my attention.

I sat up and sniffed and I, too, definitely smelled smoke.

I turned on the light and we saw a gray haze on the far side of the room coming from underneath our door.

After our little roll in the hay, we were both too spent to get up and put our jammies on, so we were both buck nekkid as our room filled with smoke.

"Quick!" I said, "Throw on a robe. We've got to get out of here before we're overcome."

We threw on our Holland-America robes and headed for the door. I turned the handle and gave it a pull, but it wouldn't budge and the smoke was getting thicker by the second.

I braced my foot against the wall and gave another tug, nearly pulling my arms out of joint.

It's stuck --- or somebody's locked it from the outside," I said. "We need to look for another way out."

"The window!" Maggie said, jumping on the bed and throwing the curtains aside.

It was obvious right away that the tiny window in the cabin was made for looking and not escaping. There was no way to open it.

Just then, I heard a loud crash from the adjoining room, and a 'thump', 'thump', 'thump'. Ox was beating on our wall.

"Walt! Can you hear me? Our cabin's filled with smoke and the door won't open!"

I thumped back and yelled, "Us, too!"

Maggie was coughing and the tears were streaming from her eyes from the acrid smoke.

"Get down on the floor away from the door," I yelled. "Smoke rises."

Maggie hit the deck and I looked around for something --- anything to get us out of this mess.

Then I thought of the shower curtain rod.

I ran into the bathroom, jerked the curtain off of the rod and pulled the rod with all my strength.

The screws popped out of the wallboard and I had a battering ram in my hands.

"Get back from the bed," I said. "I don't know where the broken glass might land."

When Maggie was safely back, I hurled the rod at the window just as I remembered how my old hero, Tarzan, had done it with his spear in the movies.

The rod bounced back on the bed, but there was a spider-web crack in the glass.

A second heave and the window shattered into a bazillion pieces. I pulled the glass-covered sheets off the bed and grabbed Maggie.

The shattering of the window had created a draft and the smoke was billowing onto the deck outside.

I threw the curtain rod out the window and said, "I'll go first and then I'll help you out."

She nodded.

I stuck my head out of the window and saw the sharp glass shards on the deck below that would cut our bare feet to ribbons.

"Hand me some pillows,"

I tossed three pillows onto the deck and went through head-first.

As soon as I was on my feet, I reached in and lifted Maggie to safety.

I could hear Ox still beating on the wall.

I pounded on his window, "Get away from the window! Can you hear me?"

"I hear you," he replied, "but whatever you're

going to do, do it quickly!"

I hit Ox's window as I had my own and it shattered on the third blow. Smoke poured from his room as it had from ours.

I could hear coughing coming from inside. "I'm sending Judy out first. I'll be right behind her."

"No you won't," I heard Judy reply. "Have you looked at the size of that window?"

It hadn't occurred to me that Ox's king-sized body might not go through the hole.

"You go first," Judy ordered. "Walt can pull from outside and I'll push from in here. Now go!"

I watched as Ox's big frame filled the window.

He stuck his arms out first, followed by his head and then his shoulders. I thought we were home free until we came to his gut. He was wedged tight and wouldn't budge.

"Suck it in, fat boy," I heard Judy yell.

Ox took a deep breath and moaned, "I shouldn't have eaten that extra chili dog."

"Let's do it on three," Judy said. "You pull and I'll push. Ox, SUCK IT IN!"

"One --- two --- three!"

It all happened at once. I pulled, Judy pushed, Ox sucked it in and let it all out of the other end.

I heard the "PLLLLLLLPPPPPTTTT" as the gaseous vapors exited Ox's backside.

His gut contracted like air rushing out of a balloon. I heard Judy mutter, "Good Lord!" and Ox's momentum carried him out the window and squarely on top of me. Unfortunately, the big guy was pretty much naked too.

It was about that time that Alejandro Reyes and his security team came hustling around the corner.

The first words out of his mouth when he saw two semi-nude men locked in an embrace on the Lower Promenade deck was, "Mr. Williams, I think it's time we had a talk!"

Reyes took the four of us to one of the security rooms.

While we sat wrapped in our terry robes, Reyes was on his walkie-talkie.

After he signed off, he approached us with a serious expression. "It seems that someone disabled the smoke alarms in both of your rooms and in the corridor and then sealed your doors with a bead of J-B Weld. After the weld had time to harden, they set the fires in front of your doors. Someone just tried to kill the four of you and I think you know why! Talk to me!"

At this point, things were so far out of hand I knew Reyes wouldn't buy another stall, so we told him the whole story.

When I had finished, he just sat motionless for the longest time. I could tell that he was fuming, but he was trying his best to stay calm.

"So let me get this straight," he said. "The four of you, including three police officers, knew that the Stewarts were on a treasure hunt for gold, that the people that occupied their former cabin had been murdered, that the perpetrators were still on my ship and you didn't bother to tell me?"

"In our defense," I replied, "we really didn't know for sure until today when they were pushed off of a cliff, that they were the actual targets, and, if you recall, on the day when the people in cabin #415 were killed, I offered our assistance and you basically told me to get lost."

He thought for a moment, "Yes, I suppose that I did. So here we are. It's quite obvious that the murderers are still on board and that they have some pretty sophisticated equipment in order to get into your cabins. Any ideas?"

I looked at my watch. "We're supposed to meet this Quimbey fellow in just a few hours to go with him on this wild goose chase. The Stewarts and Quimby have never met, so my guess is that the perps were going to kill the Stewarts, meet Quimby in their place, and if gold was actually found, whack the old guy and make off with the gold."

"I'm with you so far," he said.

"The hitch in their plan was that the Stewarts were moved and they snuffed the wrong people. Then we got involved and that complicated things for them. After they made their move on the mountain today and we pulled the Stewarts to safety, they probably figured that we had to be taken out of the picture if they were going to have a chance at the gold."

"But since you're still in the picture," he asked, "any thoughts as to what they might try next?"

"Since we meet Quimby in just a few hours," I replied, "it's probably too late for them to try to take the Stewart's place, but I certainly think you need to have someone watch our cabins until morning."

"Agreed."

"With the seven of us together, I don't think that they will try anything tomorrow while we're actually hunting for the gold. If, by some miracle, we do strike it rich, their next move will probably come when the gold is on board ship and we're out to sea. If that's the case, I think we can be ready for them."

"I'm certainly open to suggestions," he replied.

I outlined my plan and Reyes agreed.

After the details had been worked out, my practical sweetie took over. "So what now? We have no windows in our cabins and everything we own smells like smoke."

"We've got you covered," Reyes replied. "You will be assigned new cabins --- unfortunately they will be inside cabins --- that's all we have left unoccupied --- and our housekeeping department with launder all of your clothing. We'll have you ready to go by morning."

We couldn't have asked for more.

As we headed to our new cabins, it occurred to me that we had almost died twice in less than twenty-four hours.

Our peaceful Alaskan cruise was turning out to be anything but peaceful!

CHAPTER 11

Day #3-Skagway, Alaska

Gentle rapping on our door awakened me. I stumbled out of bed and standing in the hall was our room steward with all of our clothing freshly laundered as promised.

I looked at my watch and I was surprised to see that it was already seven o'clock. We were supposed to meet the Stewarts in the Lido buffet at seven-fifteen and then on to meet the mysterious Alfred Quimby at eight.

We were surprised that the Stewarts were totally unaware of our brush with death just a few hours earlier. Reyes certainly knew how to keep a lid on things.

Of all of the ports of call on our cruise, I had been looking forward to Skagway the most.

It was the Dodge City and Tombstone of Alaska all rolled into one.

After gold had been discovered, the city had grown from thirty residents to over thirty thousand in just one year. The main reason was that the two main trails from the coast to the inland gold fields, the White Pass Trail and the Chilkoot Trail, both originated from here.

Saloons and brothels sprung up almost overnight to cater to the carnal desires of the stampeders. The other industry that flourished was the outfitters that supplied the food and equipment the miners would have to pack the hundreds of miles inland to the Yukon.

Like the cow towns of the old west, Skagway attracted the lawless element as well. The most notorious was Jefferson Randolph (Soapy) Smith. This clever con man arrived in Skagway in 1897 and in nine months had become the undisputed authority. The sheriff, as well as the other city officials, were in Soapy's back pocket, leaving him and his gang of three hundred to do pretty much anything they wanted.

His saloon was recognized as the unofficial 'city hall'. His rigged card games, liquor and bawdy women separated many a miner from his hard-earned gold.

It was two of Soapy's men, Slim-Jim Foster and the Reverend John Bowers that had taken the gold from John Stewart, Mark's great-great grandfather in 1898, and it was that incident that ultimately led to Soapy's death at the hand of Frank Reid, the leader of a vigilante group.

We were to meet Quimby at the Visitor's Center on State Street, just a few blocks from where the ship was docked.

At five after eight, we stepped into the Visitor's Center and looked around. The only person we saw that didn't look like a tourist was an old gentleman in a wheelchair that looked like Walter Brennan, the old character actor from TV and the movies.

Mark approached the man, "Sir, by any

chance are you Alfred Quimby?"

"I might be," he replied. "Who's asking?"

"Mark Stewart. This is my wife Amy, and these are our friends, Walt, Maggie, Ox and Judy."

Quimby gave us the once over. "Didn't know you were bringing company," he said. "That wasn't part of the plan."

"If it weren't for these fine folks," Mark replied, "we wouldn't be here at all. Someone's tried to kill us twice since we left Vancouver. It's a long story."

Quimby looked around the room, "Not here," he said. "Follow me."

The old man spun the wheelchair around and headed for the door. Ox had to jump out of the way to avoid being run over.

"Feisty old fart," he muttered as we followed him out into the street.

Quimby headed toward a big van and pushed a remote control. The van was equipped with a wheelchair lift. Without asking for help, he backed onto the lift, pushed a lever and was soon inside.

"Well don't just stand there," he said. "Get in! I want to hear this nonsense about almost being killed."

When we were all inside, he pushed another button and the outside door closed. "Okay, tell me everything."

"We took turns, with each of us sharing the incredible story from our own point of view."

When we had finished, he looked at Mark,

"Are you positive that you told no one?"

"Absolutely!" Mark said, crossing his heart.

"Well damn!" he said. "That means that the leak must be on my end --- probably someone at the University --- someone with a great deal of technological expertise, according to your story."

He sat silent for a moment, then he became agitated, "Damn! Damn! Damn! I'll bet it's that Louis French in the Technology Department. I never trusted that asshole. He probably hacked my email and he certainly has the know-how to build the techno-toys you were talking about."

Now I was the one that was caught off guard. "Did you say Louis French?"

"Yep, sure did."

I looked at Maggie, "Wasn't that the guy that asked us to take his picture on the Mount Roberts Lookout?"

She thought for a moment, "Yes, I'm sure that it was. That was just a diversion, wasn't it?"

"So it would seem," I replied. He saw Ox and Judy heading for the can and delayed us just long enough for his partners in crime to push Mark and Amy off the cliff."

"That son-of-a-bitch," Quimby muttered. "I'll strangle the bastard with my bare hands!"

It appeared that Quimby was indeed as salty as an old sailor!

"So what now?" Mark asked. "Are we still going after the gold? Is it really worth putting our lives at risk?"

"Hell, yes, we're going after the gold!" Quimby retorted. "This doesn't change anything other than we just need to keep our eyes open."

His eyes took on a far away look, "Just think! Your great-great grandfather did something that tens of thousands tried to do and failed --- he braved the hardships of the Yukon and found gold. A hundred and fourteen years ago, that hard-earned gold was taken from him by two of the most notorious thieves in Alaska. After Soapy Smith was killed because of that gold, the two rats that robbed John Stewart took off for the White Pass Trail, but were caught. The gold was never found. Today, John Stewart's great-great grandson is going to find that gold. It will be one of those rare moments in history where things come full circle --- so, hell yes we're going after that gold!"

It was obvious to everyone that Quimby was going, with or without us, and quite frankly, when he was talking, the hair stood up on the back of my neck. We were going to experience a real piece of history and go on a real, honest-to-goodness treasure hunt and I was as excited as a six-year-old kid at Christmas!

Mark brought things back into the present. "You said in your email that you had found a document that tells where the gold was buried. Was it a map?"

"Not exactly a map in the true sense of the word," Quimby said, "but a map of sorts."

I saw the skeptical look on Mark's face.

Quimby opened a briefcase and pulled out a yellowed scrap of paper. "This was in a box of things that the Juneau Prison sent to the University."

He handed the paper to Mark. We all peered over his shoulder.

In faded letters were scrawled these words:

The love of my life has golden hair
And though I'm gone she should not despair.
For she shall not be left alone
She'll be in the care of one unknown.

And while I'm gone, she'll have to wait
Just inside the wooden gate.
The falls will be her closest friend
Just up the path and around the bend.

Then one day soon I will return
To the golden girl for whom I yearn.
We'll be together as before
And want for nothing evermore.

Rev. J. Bowers

"That's it?" Mark said, incredulously. "I came all this way and risked our lives for that?"

Poor Quimby looked like Mark had slapped him across the face.

"It does look pretty poetic for a shyster con-man," Maggie observed. "Sounds like something Poe would write."

"The Reverend Bowers was more that just a con man," Quimby said indignantly. "He was quite articulate."

Quimby snatched the paper away from Mark, "Follow along with me here. The references to 'golden hair' and the 'golden girl' are pretty self-explanatory. He was talking about gold --- no doubt!"

I could see that Mark was still not convinced.

Quimby forged ahead, "The second verse gives us clues as to the location where he buried the gold. We know he and Slim-Jim were headed north out of town and they were captured before they had gone too far, and I can think of one place about two and a half miles north of town that fits the clues --- the old Gold Rush Cemetery. There used to be a wooden fence and gate around the cemetery, but it has rotted away, and just beyond the cemetery, 'up the path and around the bend' is Reid Falls."

"So what are we supposed to do?" Mark said, "Dig up the whole cemetery?"

"Not at all," Quimby replied with a sly smile. "The last remaining clue will show us exactly where to dig. Let's get rolling!"

The van had been equipped for a handicapped driver with controls on the steering column. Quimby rolled his chair into position, locked the wheels and hit the ignition. In just a few moments we were cruising through town.

"Would you be offended if I asked you about your handicap?" Amy asked.

"Heavens no!" Quimby replied. "It happened

about five years ago. I had come across some information that led me to an abandoned mine --- and gold, of course --- but rotted support timbers gave way and buried me under a pile of rock and debris. They dug me out and saved my life, but I've been like this ever since. It's a damn drag, I'm telling you."

It looked like we had come face-to-face with a real, live Indiana Jones.

It didn't take long to get to the Gold Rush Cemetery just north of town. *

The place gave me the creeps the moment that I saw it. It looked exactly like the cemeteries depicted in the old zombie and vampire movies. Instead of the neat rows of granite tombstones that I was accustomed to seeing in Kansas City, there seemed to be no logical order to this place. Old wooden grave markers with names and dates scrawled in black paint were scattered among giant trees as old as the graves themselves. The dense, dark forest in the background created an eerie sense of mystery and foreboding.

Hardly a word was spoken as we walked the gravel path between the graves. Most of the occupants appeared to have died in the late eighteen hundreds, but a few were inscribed in the early nineteen hundreds.

Mark was the first to discover the final resting place of the infamous Soapy Smith. His plot and grave marker were enclosed behind a wooden fence.*

* See photo on page 220
* See photo on page 221

I had read dozens of stories about this notorious outlaw and at the time, they seemed like just that --- stories, but actually seeing his grave made it all come alive for me.

It was like I had stepped back in time a hundred years and my imagination was reliving the events that led to his untimely death when Quimby jolted me back into the present.

"Okay, enough lolly-gagging! We've got work to do!"

"Fair enough," Mark said. "You told us that you had one more clue that would tell us where the gold might be buried. Care to share that with us now?"

Quimby smiled and pulled the ancient scrap of paper from his shirt pocket.

"Second verse," he said. *"For she shall not be left alone, she'll be in the care of one unknown.* Look around and tell me if you see something that might relate to this verse."

We drifted apart and began looking for anything that would relate to the curious clue.

Amy spotted it first. "Here! This has to be it!"

We gathered around and looked at what had captured her attention.

There, among the moss covered roots of a huge tree was a grave marker with the inscription, "Unknown". *

---

* See photo on page 222

Quimby looked like the cat that had swallowed the canary. "See! He left his golden girl with one unknown. I knew it!"

"Yeah," Ox said, pointing to another marker twenty feet away, "but which 'unknown'?" *

We looked, and sure enough, there was another one.

Quimby was undeterred, "So? We dig two holes. I see several strong backs and I've brought plenty of shovels. They're in the back of the van. Hop to it!"

With equipment in hand, Ox and I tackled one grave while Mark dug into the other.

As I turned over the first shovel full of dirt, a thought occurred to me. "Is this even legal?"

"Darned if I know," Ox replied. "If someone comes along and says it's not, we can plead ignorance."

"I've seen movies of creepy guys digging up graves," I said. "I think they're called 'ghouls'."

"Well, if that's the case," Ox said with a grin, "you're definitely the 'ghoul of my dreams'."

"Very funny!"

My back was starting to ache, so I handed the shovel off to my tag team partner.

As we dug, Quimby was busy snapping photos of the whole operation for his next historical paper.

---

* See photo on page 222

The hole was about three feet wide and two feet deep when Ox's shovel hit something solid and metallic sounding.

"We've either struck gold or the guy's casket," Ox said.

That brought everyone running.

We traded the big spade for a hand trowel and gently removed the dirt from around the obstacle that Ox had hit. It turned out to be a metal box about the size of a loaf of bread.

When it was loose, he sat it on the edge of the grave. "Feels heavy enough," Ox said.

The box had a lid, but it was rusted shut.

"Screwdriver," Quimby said impatiently, "in the toolbox in the van."

Mark retrieved the screwdriver and handed it to Quimby. "Here, you do the honors. This is your moment of glory. I'll take your picture as you open the box."

Quimby took the screwdriver with trembling hands. This was a moment that he had waited for his entire life.

After considerable effort, the top popped open revealing a bag that was made from the hide of some animal. It was held shut by a piece of rawhide.

I had seen photos of John Stewart holding his bag of gold and the thing in the box looked like the real thing.

Quimby lifted the bag out of the metal box and started working on the rawhide knot. It crumbled with his first tug. It was, after all, over a hundred years old.

He opened the pouch and I heard him gasp as he looked inside.

"Well," Mark asked, "is it there?"

Quimby didn't answer. He simply reached into the poke and pulled out a golden nugget the size of a marble.

"Holy Crap!" Ox said.

I think that pretty much summed up what we were all feeling.

I looked at Mark and tears were streaming down his cheeks. "So it's true! My great-great grandfather --- my very own flesh and blood --- filled that pouch with his own blood, sweat and tears. It's like a family heirloom that's been hidden away for generations. Thank you --- thanks to all of you that have helped make this possible."

Amy slid her arms around his waist and hugged him tight.

Quimby, Mr. Practical, had some sound advice.

"We'd better get these holes filled and get out of here. Tourists come up here all the time and I don't want to have to explain why we're robbing graves."

No one argued.

Back in the privacy of the van, Quimby snapped more photos, then handed the bag of gold to Mark. "I have what I came for and now you do too. It's all yours. When my paper is published, I'll send you a copy."

In the excitement and thrill of the moment, the fact that we had all nearly been killed over that bag of gold was conveniently forgotten, but as we headed back to town, there was no escaping the possibility that we were in even more danger now that the gold was actually in our hands.

It was time to set our plan in motion and hope for the best.

In the rail yard that bordered the old cemetery, three figures watched as the treasure hunters dug into the unmarked graves.

It was obvious that they had found something, and when they heard the big one shout "Holy Crap!" they knew that the gold was really there.

"The old fool actually found it," Louis French said. "Now the question is, how are we going to make it ours?"

"Do you think they'll put it in the ship's safe?" Gwen asked.

"It's possible, but I'm betting 'no'," French replied. "The ship's company is composed almost entirely of foreigners and once that gold leaves the Stewart's hands there could be all kinds of complications getting it back. Let's face it. People are greedy --- just like us. If I were Mark Stewart, I would hide the gold away and not tell a soul. There's a safe in each of the ship's cabins, and I'm betting that Stewart will lock the gold up there."

"So what's next?" Luke asked.

"According to their itinerary, they're all supposed to go on the White Pass Railroad up to Fraser, British Columbia, and return to Skagway by bus. That's a twenty-seven mile trip up the mountain. If you tag along, you might find another opportunity to eliminate some of the obstacles that are keeping us from that gold, if you get my drift."

"So what will you be doing while we're traipsing up the mountain?" Luke asked.

"We're still a long way from Anchorage where the Stewarts and the gold are to board a plane back to Missouri. I'll be doing some shopping just in case we can't get our hands on the gold tomorrow on the trip to Glacier Bay. Are you all set for tomorrow?"

"Yes, we know what to do," Luke replied. "While everyone is on deck gawking at the stupid icebergs, we'll search their cabin for the gold, but we'll have to be very careful. I think the old cop is suspicious of us."

"Maybe if you're lucky, he won't be alive tomorrow to get in your way!"

It was about eleven-thirty when the van pulled up on the wharf.

We were all supposed to board the White Pass Railroad for a trip up the mountain and our group was to board the bus to the railroad depot at twelve-thirty. We just had time to eat a bite of lunch in the Lido buffet and grab our passports.

I was surprised when Mark handed me the bag of gold. "Walt, I'd like you to take this to Mr. Reyes for safekeeping."

"So what are you going to do?" I asked. "Aren't you going on the train?"

"No," he replied. "Amy and I are going to have lunch with Mr. Quimby. Because of his research, he knows so much about my great-great grandfather and I want to know it all. It's like I'm just getting to know something about my roots. I may never have this opportunity again, and besides, we have some shopping to do if we're going to lay our trap for the thieves. You all go and have a good time."

I had really been looking forward to this excursion.

The first prospectors to head north to the Yukon from Skagway took the White Pass Trail. It was a twenty-mile journey from sea level to the summit at three thousand feet, which marked the border between Alaska and British Columbia.

The Canadian authorities wouldn't let the miners go further without adequate supplies that would weigh nearly a ton. The only way up was by foot and the hardy souls made multiple trips up and down the trail in the dead of winter, fighting blizzards and temperatures of sixty below zero, with hundred pound packs on their backs.

Once their provisions were at the summit, it was another twenty miles along the White Pass Trail to the shores of Lake Bennet where they would have to construct boats to carry them on the next leg of their journey. From there, it was still over five hundred miles to the Yukon gold fields.

I couldn't begin to imagine the hardships they faced and the physical torture that they endured to satisfy their lust for gold.

It had been estimated that over a hundred thousand men and women headed north, and of that number, between thirty and forty thousand actually reached the gold fields, and of that number, maybe four thousand actually found gold and only a few hundred became rich.

Not very good odds.

In 1898, some enterprising fellows decided to build a railroad along the White Pass Trail.

Given the fact that the bed for the tracks had to be hewn out of the side of the mountain, they decided on a narrow gauge railroad. The rails were a mere three feet apart on a ten-foot wide roadbed.

Dynamite had not yet come to Alaska, so over four hundred and fifty tons of black powder explosives were used to blast away the mountain. Tens of thousands of men worked on the construction gang, many of which were suspended by ropes to plant the explosive charges.

Construction began in May of 1898. They worked through the harsh winter and had reached the summit by February of 1899 and the shores of Lake Bennet by July of 1899. A fantastic feat!

We were to ride the train twenty-seven miles to Fraser, British Columbia, board a bus to take us back to Skagway via the Klondike Highway, with a stop at Liarsville, just outside of the city.

Being a narrow gauge railroad, the cars were not wide. Two passengers could sit on either side of a narrow aisle. It was definitely smaller in width than the airplane that had brought us north.

All of the seats faced the engine end of the train. Upon reaching Fraser, the seats would be reversed, the engines would be moved to what was formerly the rear of the train and the whole kit and kaboodle would go back down the mountain with the passengers that had been brought up the mountain on the busses. We would just be trading places with them. What a system!

When the train started chugging out of town, the first landmark that we passed was the Gold Rush Cemetery. A conductor-type person had been giving us a running commentary on the town and the railroad since we left the station.

As I listened to him tell the story of Soapy Smith, who's grave we had seen there, I couldn't help but smile. Only a few hours before, another piece of history had been unearthed there and we had been part of it. Maybe when our little adventure was over and the news of the gold had been published by Quimby, our exploits would become part of his daily banter.

It was an incredible trip up the mountain.

As I looked out the window, I could see the mountain rising almost vertically on one side and the river hundreds of feet below on the other. The tracks on the narrow roadbed seemed to be suspended in mid-air. I couldn't help but marvel at such an engineering feat, built a hundred and fourteen years ago with the most primitive of tools.

At one point, the conductor said that if we looked directly below, we could see remnants of the original White Pass Trail.

We craned our necks and saw a tiny path, maybe three feet wide along the edge of the cliff.

The conductor said that the trail had become known as the 'Dead Horse Trail' because over three thousand horses had died trying to carry the prospector's supplies up the mountain.

As I looked at the tiny path, another thought occurred to me. John Stewart had trod that same path years ago, braving the hardships of the Alaskan winter on his six hundred mile journey to the gold fields, and had returned the same way carrying a bag of gold that I had held in my hands just a few hours earlier.

A tear ran down my cheek as I envisioned the journey of that hardy pioneer.

We had been snapping pictures furiously. Around every bend were waterfalls and other natural wonders. The conductor announced that we were approaching the sixteen-mile marker and the first of two tunnels that had been dug through the side of the mountain. At that point, we were a thousand feet above the floor of the gulch. *

He warned us that once in the tunnel, we would be engulfed in total darkness.

The approach to the tunnel was a sharp hairpin turn that gave us a fantastic photo opportunity of the engine entering the gaping hole in the mountain.

The conductor was right. Once inside, it was dark as pitch. It took maybe thirty seconds from one end of the tunnel to the other.

He informed us that we would be coming up to the second tunnel, which was even longer, in two miles.

I decided that I wanted to get a clearer photo of the next tunnel and announced that I was going to go out to the platform for a better shot.

Maggie wasn't so sure. "Walt, that could be dangerous. The way the train is jerking back and forth, you could fall."

---

* See photo on page 223

I supposed that was a possibility because the railroad had published the warning in their safety tips, "*Ride on platforms at your own risk*".

I had seen others come and go to the platforms without incident, and besides, if the hardy souls of yesteryear could hike the mountain in the dead of winter, I ought to be able to at least hang onto a platform.

Ox announced that he was going with me. He needed some air and also wanted some pictures.

When we stepped out onto the platform, the cool mountain air was quite a shock. The sun had been shining brightly, so we had only worn light jackets. After all, we were only going to be inside a train and then on a bus.

We were in the second car from the engine and there were four more cars behind ours, all filled with tourists just like us.

The approach to the second tunnel wasn't as dramatic as the first. There was no hairpin turn so I had to lean far out over the platform to get a shot of the engine entering the tunnel. The train slowed down to a crawl so that everyone on board could record the moment for posterity.

Ox crowded in beside me and together we snapped away until we were engulfed in darkness.

"Ohhh, this is really creepy," Ox said.

The words were barely out of his mouth when I heard the door of the car behind us snap shut.

I was about to ask who was there when a hand grabbed the back of my jacket and lifted me over the top of the rail. I could feel Ox being manhandled at the same time.

It was only an instant that I was suspended on the edge, but it felt like an eternity. Then there was a shove and I felt myself falling into the black void.

The train picked up speed as it exited the tunnel.

Judy turned to Maggie, "Our shutterbugs should be returning soon. They must be freezing their butts off out there."

"Can't have that," Maggie quipped. "Walt doesn't have any butt to spare."

Another few minutes passed.

"Maybe we should check on them," Judy said. "Sometimes I don't think Ox has enough sense to come in from out in the cold."

"You're probably right," Maggie replied. "The last thing we need is for them to come down with a cold and spend the rest of the trip sneezing and coughing."

They went to the back of the car and looked out onto the empty platform.

"What gives?" Judy asked.

"Maybe they went into one of the other cars," Maggie offered.

"The safety rules said, *'Passengers are prohibited from crossing aprons while the train is in motion'*. I remember Ox reading that to me."

"Have rules ever stopped our guys before?" Maggie replied. "Remember, we dug up two graves just a few hours ago."

"You've got a point," Judy said.

Gingerly, they stepped across the apron connecting the two cars and went inside. No Ox and no Walt.

"Now I'm getting worried," Judy said.

Just then a conductor came up the aisle. "You really should return to your seats while the train is moving," he said.

"I'm not going anywhere until we find our husbands!" Judy replied indignantly.

The conductor looked perplexed. "You --- uhhh ---- both lost husbands?"

"They went out onto the observation platform just before we reached the second tunnel and we haven't seen them since."

Now the conductor was getting concerned. "What are their names? I'll call them over the intercom and ask them to return to their seats. Okay?"

Judy and Maggie returned to their seats and moments later they heard the announcement over the intercom.

"Your attention, please. Will passengers Walter Williams and George Wilson please return to your seats."

Minutes passed and there was still no sign of them.

The conductor returned, "We're almost to the summit. We'll have to stop there so that Canadian customs can check everyone's passport. We'll search all of the cars while we're stopped."

Once the train came to a halt, it was twenty minutes before the conductor returned. "I'm sorry. We have searched every car. Mr. Williams and Mr. Wilson are just not on board."

"Then we'll just have to go back to the tunnel," Maggie said with tears in her eyes. "That's the last place that we saw them."

"I'm afraid that's not possible," the conductor said. "It's seven more miles to Fraser where the engines will move to the rear of the train. We'll pick up the bus passengers and then head back to Skagway. We'll watch for your husbands on the way back."

"You damn right you will," Judy said, getting in the man's face, "because we're coming with you!"

"Aren't you supposed to board one of the busses?" he asked.

"If you think we're going to go tooling down the Klondike Highway while our husbands are somewhere out on those tracks, you're crazy. We're coming with you! End of story! Any objections?"

The conductor saw the fire in Judy's eyes. "Uhhhh --- no objections. I think we can work it out."

Thankfully, the train was barely moving and it was just a few feet from the platform to the roadbed.

Ox hit the gravel first and I landed squarely on top of him. Reflecting back, I'm thankful that the opposite did not occur.

I heard the air leave his body in a big 'WHOOSH' as I made contact with his midsection.

Our momentum had carried us to the inside wall of the tunnel which was a mere couple of feet from the rails where the train was picking up speed.

We pressed our backs against the wall and watched the sparks flying from the wheels as they passed over the iron rails.

After the train had passed, we laid still in the darkness.

Finally, I said, "Ox, are you okay?"

"Don't know," he replied. "I'm afraid to move."

I felt my body parts and everything seemed to still be attached and functional.

I struggled to my feet and suddenly everything hurt. I supposed that was a normal occurrence after being thrown off of a moving train.

I heard Ox moan in the darkness as he

stumbled to his feet. "I --- I think I can walk, but which way?"

I could see the light from the way we had come, but the other direction was utter darkness.

"Let's walk toward the light," I suggested.

"Isn't that what people say right after they've died?"

At least his sense of humor was still intact.

We trudged toward the tunnel entrance and when we emerged it took a few minutes for our eyes to adapt to the light.

Ox gave me the once-over. "You look like crap!"

"You're not exactly the picture of health yourself," I replied.

Our clothes were torn and red splotches were seeping through from our cuts and scratches.

"Coulda been worse," he said. "I'm guessing that whoever pitched us overboard was hoping that we'd be crushed under the wheels."

"Do you suppose that the 'whoever' was our gold hungry friends hoping to get us out of the way so that they would have an easier go at the Stewarts?"

"That would be my guess," he replied, "unless you've made some enemies on the cruise that I don't know about."

"So what now?" I asked. "The map showed that the second tunnel was about halfway between Fraser and Skagway. I don't see us walking either direction." Just then a gust of wind sent a chill through my body. "I'm certainly not crazy about spending a night here on the mountain. With these light jackets, we'd freeze to death."

"Didn't we hear that the train comes back down the mountain from Fraser after picking up the bus passengers? Ox asked. "Maybe we can hitch a ride back."

Then it hit me. "Bus passengers! Maggie! Judy! They must be going nuts!"

"Oh, Lordy!" he replied. "I wouldn't want to be on that train right now. Judy will be tearing the place apart!"

"So how do we stop a moving train?" I asked. "I'm not real big on standing on the tracks waving my arms." I looked over the edge of the roadbed to the river hundreds of feet below. "If they don't see us and stop, there's not much wiggle room here."

"Let's build a fire," he said. "Right in the middle of the track. It would be hard to miss the smoke billowing up in front of them."

"So what do you propose, rubbing two sticks together?"

"I have something more modern in mind," he said, removing a lighter from his pocket.

The lighter had a picture of a scantily clad lady with the inscription, "Let me light your fire."

"Cute!" I said.

"I picked it up at one of the tourist traps in Ketchikan," he said. "I got it for Dooley back at the precinct. I figured that he would appreciate the art work."

"Works for me!"

We gathered sticks that had fallen on the mountainside of the roadbed and scooped up handfuls of dead pine needles. I put the wood together just like I remembered from my Boy Scout days, Ox flicked his Bic, and soon we had a roaring fire going. The warmth felt wonderful and we settled in to wait for the train. All we needed now was a bag of marshmallows.

Suddenly, I realized something was wrong --- there was no smoke. The old dried stuff was burning cleanly. "We need green stuff," I said.

Once again, I was glad I had Ox. The big guy reached up to the lowest hanging boughs and snapped off leafy branches. Once we had a nice pile, we settled in again.

Several hours had passed before something told me that the train was not that far away. Because it would be coming out of the tunnel, we wouldn't actually see it until it was right on top of us.

Then I remembered a scene from an old cowboy movie and I placed my ear against the rail.

"Train coming!" I muttered.

"Who do you think you are? Tonto?" Ox asked.

"You try it!"

He put his ear to the rail. "Yep! Train coming!"

We heaped the green boughs on our fire and gray smoke billowed into the sky.

We could only hope that our smoke signal said, "STOP!"

We stood in front of the fire wildly waving our arms as the train emerged from the tunnel. We had made sure that there was sufficient room on the mountainside of the tracks just in case the engineer wasn't paying attention. *

Apparently he was, because as soon as the engine cleared the opening, the big wheels locked and the train came to a screeching halt.

Maggie and Judy hopped off and came running. They threw themselves into our arms and held us tight.

Maggie was sobbing uncontrollably and Judy was trying to put on a brave front but finally couldn't hold back.

After the waterworks had subsided, Maggie held me at arms length. "Are you okay?"

"I'll live."

"How about you?" Judy asked.

"Guess I'll live too," Ox replied.

"Well, you both look like crap!" she said. "We can't take you guys anywhere!"

We had to laugh because we just couldn't cry anymore.

---

* See photo on page 223

CHAPTER 12

"That's just not possible," Luke said as he watched the two cops and their wives cross the wharf and head to the Statendam. "We've pushed them off of a cliff, set fire to their cabins and tossed them off of a moving train, and they just keep coming back!"

Louis French smiled, "Just like Timex watches --- they take a licking and keep on ticking."

Then, the smile faded. "You have two more days at sea to get the job done. If you fail, then it will be up to me when they reach Seward. If you fail again and I have to finish the job, you're both out! Do you understand?"

They both nodded.

"Undoubtedly, they will put the gold into the wall safe in their room. It can't be very sophisticated because there are hundreds of them on the ship. I have devised this piece of equipment to help you open the safe," he said, handing them a device with a stethoscope-like attachment. "Take this to your cabin and practice on your own safe until you are proficient. When the opportunity arises, you should have no trouble with the tools that I have given you.

This is your last chance. Don't disappoint me again!"

Even though Ox and I were dirty, cut, bruised and tired, we figured that our first stop should be with Alejandro Reyes and the Stewarts to make sure that everything was in place before we set sail from Skagway.

Maggie called the Stewarts and asked them to meet us at Reyes' security room.

We were the first to arrive and when Reyes opened the door, his first comment was, "What happened to the two of you. You look like crap!"

That seemed to be the general consensus.

The Stewarts arrived at that moment, so we spent the next fifteen minutes sharing our White Pass Railroad story.

Ox was quick to point out that my injuries would probably have been more severe had he not hit the roadbed first to cushion my fall. I really couldn't argue the point.

"Any idea who tossed you off?" Reyes asked.

"None," Ox replied. "It was pitch black and there were hundreds of people on that train."

Then a thought occurred to me. "I wonder if Luke and Gwen Larson were aboard?"

Reyes went to the computer and tapped the keys. "As a matter of fact, they were."

"What a coincidence," Judy observed.

"Sorry," I replied, "I don't believe in

coincidence. I think they're Louis French's partners in crime --- we just don't have the evidence to prove it."

"Maybe we will soon," Judy said, turning to the Stewarts. "Was your shopping trip a success?"

"Indeed it was," Mark replied. "We added Alejandro's little surprise to our purchase and it's tucked away in our safe."

"So," I said, "now we wait and hope for the best."

We were almost back to our cabins when we realized that we had left the bags that we had taken on our excursion in Reyes' security room.

"Well, crap!" I said, "one of us will have to go back."

"I'll flip you for it," Ox said with an innocent smile.

"No need. I might as well just go."

"No, no. It's the only fair thing to do," he said, pulling a quarter from his pocket. "Call it," he said, flipping it into the air.

My first instinct was 'tails', but then I remembered that I always get it wrong, so at the last moment, I blurted, "Heads!"

Naturally, it came up 'tails'.

"Tails," Ox said, shaking his head. "What are the chances?"

"Fifty-fifty, my ass!" I muttered as I trudged back down the hall.

After a long, hot shower and a back-rub by my sweetie, I almost felt human again.

We dressed and met our four friends in the Rotterdam Dining Room. Any other night, I would have lobbied for the Lido Buffet, but I had to admit that it felt really good to just sit and let Den and Mukti wait on us.

After dinner, we headed to the Showroom Theatre for Bob Mackie's production of *Broadway*.

We had really enjoyed the entertainment each evening and that night was no exception.

The band and the singers belted out favorite tunes from the Broadway musicals and two, very lovely dancers, Kristin and Lizzie cavorted across the stage in skimpy costumes.

At the end of the performance, when the Cruise Director was introducing all of the performers, he made mention that the two, leggy dancers would be in the Crow's Nest at ten o'clock the next day to teach anyone interested how to waltz.

Maggie and I were already accomplished ballroom dancers, so we didn't pay much attention, but when Judy heard the announcement, her ears perked up.

"Oh, Ox," she pleaded, "you know how much I've wanted to learn to dance. Could we go?"

I saw the look of terror register on Ox's face, but to his credit, he simply said, "Sure, Judy. If it would make you happy."

I elbowed Maggie and said, "I wouldn't miss this for all the salmon in Alaska!"

CHAPTER 13

Day #4-Glacier Bay

With the exception of the first day in Ketchikan, we had been blessed with fantastic weather. For the past two days, the sky had been sunny and the temperature had hovered in the low sixties. We were hoping for the same for our trip through Glacier Bay.

When I awoke, the cabin was dark. Then I remembered that we had been moved to an inside cabin. I threw on my robe and walked to the door leading to the Lower Promenade Deck. I was thrilled to see the bright rays of the sun peeking over the mountaintops.

We hurriedly dressed and met our friends in the Lido Buffet.

By eight o'clock, we were outside on the forward deck, wrapped in blankets in the warm sun, sipping on hot chocolate as we watched the beautiful Alaskan wilderness pass by on both sides of the ship.

Captain George Vancouver had visited the bay over two hundred years earlier, and since his visit, due to changes in the climate, several of the glaciers that he saw had receded out of view. Still there were nine tidewater glaciers within the park.

The bay itself was sixty-five miles long with mountains, fjords and inlets on both sides.

Every so often, someone would let out a yelp and everyone would run to where the person was pointing, and most often it was some wildlife. The pod of Orca whales swimming along side the ship was my favorite.

The time passed quickly, and this was actually the first day of our cruise that someone's life had not been in danger.

Ox had been drifting in and out of short catnaps as he soaked up the morning sun. Our peaceful reverie was interrupted when Judy announced, "Oh, look! It's almost ten o'clock! We just have time to get to the Crow's Nest for our waltz lesson!"

Suddenly Ox's daydreams had turned into a nightmare. I'm sure he had been hoping that Judy would be so engrossed in the beauty of Glacier Bay that she would forget about the waltz, but it wasn't to be.

For a brute of a man that is fearless in the face of physical danger, Ox is totally petrified of most social situations.

As much as he had been smitten the first time he had seen Judy, it was like pulling teeth to get him to approach her, and in the end, she was the one that asked him on their first date.

In spite of the cool weather, beads of perspiration were appearing on Ox's forehead as we rode the elevator to the Crow's Nest.

The Crow's Nest was the ship's nightclub located on deck twelve at the very tip-top of the ship. It consisted of a full service bar, a DJ booth and a small dance floor. There had been something going on there every evening after the main stage show, but we had all been so frazzled after our near-death experiences, all we wanted to do was hit the sack.

When we arrived, Kristin and Lizzie and a dozen other couples were already there.

Mark and Amy found an empty spot and Judy dragged Ox to another one. Maggie and I found chairs with a good view of the dance floor.

Kristen started things off. "The waltz is an easy dance. If you can count to three, you can waltz."

I knew Ox could count to three, but I was willing to bet that it would be anything but easy for him.

They put all of the men one side and the women on the other. Kristin then showed the men their steps.

"Watch what I do. You will lead with your left foot --- forward, side, together --- that is your first step. Then you will lead with your right foot --- back, side, together. That brings you back to your original position and you just do the whole thing all over again. Now you try it."

She led the count --- forward, side, together --- but of course, Ox went forward, together, side --- and he was screwed from the first step.

Next, Lizzie went over the women's part that was just the opposite of the men's.

Then, it was time to partner up. Kristin and Lizzie demonstrated the partnership hold, and counted off the first steps.

Judy led with her right foot back, but

unfortunately so did Ox, and his 230 pounds landed squarely on Judy's left foot.

"Owww! Son-of-a-bitch!" she yelped as she limped away.

That brought the lesson to a halt and I could see that Ox wanted to crawl into a hole somewhere.

I leaned over to Maggie, "Shall we rescue our friends?"

"It's the only decent thing to do," she replied. "You work with Ox and I'll help Judy."

We dragged our friends off of the floor to an open area behind the bar. I could tell that Kristen was happy to see them go.

When I got Ox by himself, I said, "I'm only doing this because you let me land on you yesterday."

"Very funny!"

For the next fifteen minutes, I coached the big guy. At first, it was like trying to push a rope or herd cats, but he finally got the hang of it. By the time Judy and Maggie came over, he was certainly no Fred Astaire, but at least he wasn't lethal.

I noticed when they returned to the dance floor, the other dancers gave them a wide berth.

By this time, everyone else was dancing to music. Lizzie queued the song and the beautiful strains of *You Light Up My Life* filled the room.

Ox started off very hesitantly, but Judy was patient and supportive, and before long, they were right in step.

My partner was actually dancing, and I could

tell by the way that they were looking into each other's eyes that they had found another way to light up each other's life.

Maybe you *can* actually teach an old dog new tricks.

When the session was over, it was nearly lunchtime.

We decided that Mark and Amy should swing by their cabin to see if anyone had paid them an uninvited visit.

When we met them in the Lido for lunch, they just shook their heads. The safe had been untouched.

By the time lunch was over, the Statendam was deep inside Glacier Bay. We had noticed chunks of ice floating by, and the farther we went, the more numerous and larger they became.

We felt the ship slow to a crawl. We were nearing the Margerie Glacier. The huge chunk of ice was a mile wide at sea level, rose two hundred and fifty feet from the sea and stretched inland twenty-one miles.

Because of the glacier's sheer vertical face, there was a good possibility that we could see some 'calving', which happens when chunks of ice break off and fall into the water. We were told that a rifle-like crack and a booming roar usually accompany such an occurrence.

With the expectation of this Alaskan marvel, pretty much everyone was out on one of the decks with camera in hand.

We wrapped in our blankets and joined the

rest of the gawkers, hoping Mother Nature wouldn't disappoint.

By this time, the chunks of ice that the ship was maneuvering through were less like 'chunks' and more like small icebergs. I remembered Bernice's admonition about warning the Captain of the Titanic's fate, but figured that he been through here a time or two and probably knew what he was doing.

The ship actually came to a dead stop along side the glacier's face and remained there for about a half hour until a chunk of ice peeled away and dropped into the water. It wasn't a big chunk, but it was a chunk and we got to see it. Shortly after, the big engines started and the ship started on its return journey through the bay.

Mother Nature didn't disappoint.

Luke and Gwen Larson watched the Stewarts and the other two couples leave the Lido buffet, wrap themselves in blankets and plop down in deck chairs as the ship neared the Margerie Glacier.

"They'll probably be there at least until the ship passes the glacier and turns back toward open sea," Luke said. "Shall we do it?"

"There'll never be a better chance," Gwen replied. "I'm ready!"

They headed back to their cabin, picked up the equipment that Louis French had given them and went directly to the Stewart's cabin.

Luke slipped the card device into the slot, saw the green light and pushed the door open.

"Gotta hand it to Louis," Luke said. "He's good with the tekkie stuff."

They opened the closet door and moved aside the clothing that was hanging in front of the small safe.

Luke handed French's latest device to Gwen, who had the more sensitive ear. "Okay, you're on --- just like you practiced in our cabin. You can do this."

Gwen positioned the little plastic microphones in her ears, placed the stethoscope against the safe and began to slowly rotate the dial to the left.

"Got the first one," she said after a few moments, and then began turning the dial to the right. "Two down!" She hadn't turned it very far back to the left when she exclaimed, "Got it!"

She drew back and Luke turned the handle. The door swung open, revealing the century-old bag filled with the treasure that they had killed for.

Luke gently lifted the bag from the safe. "Heavy --- heavier than I thought it would be."

"Can we take a quick look?" Gwen asked.

"Maybe just a quick one," Luke replied, and then we'd better get out of here before they return."

Luke opened the top of the bag and they saw the gold shining from the reflection of the overhead light.

"We did it! We actually did it," she exclaimed, and gave Luke a hug.

They closed the safe, re-hung the clothing and peeked out into the hall. Seeing no one, they slipped out of the room, pulled the door closed and headed back to their own cabin.

Like Slim-Jim Foster and John Bowers a century earlier, they had just relieved a Stewart of a fortune in gold.

It was almost three o'clock before we turned in our blankets and headed back to our cabins.

We had actually stayed out on the deck longer than we normally would have, but we wanted to make sure the thieves had plenty of opportunity to make their move.

We followed the Stewarts to their cabin and the six of us crowded inside. Mark opened the closet, removed the hanging clothing and turned the dial on the safe.

We held our collective breaths as the door swung open.

"Empty!" he said. "We've got 'em!"

We hurried to Alejandro Reyes' security room and knocked.

"Well?" he said, when he opened the door and saw the six of us standing there.

"They have it," I said "Turn on your tracker."

Reyes took a small computer-looking thing with a screen off of a shelf and pushed the power button.

We watched impatiently as the thing booted up. Finally, a small red blip pulsated on the screen.

"There's the tracking device we hid in the bag. Looks like our perps are on Deck #6," he said. "Shall we have a look?"

"Try and stop us," Judy replied.

"One thing before we go," he cautioned us, "my men and I will take care of this. Remember, whoever this is, they brutally murdered two people and probably tried to kill you at least twice, so we have to consider them dangerous."

"You're the boss," I said, as we headed out the door.

Luke and Gwen Larson hurried back to their cabin. They were anxious to actually hold the precious metal in their hands. They spread a pillowcase on the bed and dumped the contents of the old hide bag.

Luke stared in disbelief at the pieces of gold that tumbled onto the bed.

"SHIT!"

"What?" Gwen asked. "Is something wrong?"

"Fool's gold! This isn't real gold --- it's iron pyrite --- fool's gold! They must have bought this stuff in one of the gem and mineral shops in Skagway."

"But why? How?" Gwen stammered.

Luke ran his fingers through the pyrite crystals. "For this!" he said, holding a small disc between his finger and thumb."

"What is it?" Gwen asked.

"A tracking device. We've been set up! We've got to get this stuff out of here. They're probably on their way right now!"

They quickly stuffed the pyrite along with the tracking device back into the bag, grabbed their jackets and headed out to the Lower Promenade Deck. When they reached the rail, Luke looked around, and seeing no one close by, tossed the bag into the sea.

"What now?" Gwen asked.

"We can't go back to the cabin right away. They may be in our hallway and we don't want them to see us. Let's walk the deck to the bow of the ship and take one of the forward elevator's to the Crow's Nest. We'll hang out there for a while. I just hope that damn tracker didn't pinpoint our cabin number. We'll know soon enough."

The six of us, along with Reyes and two security officers stepped off of the elevator on Deck #6.

Reyes looked at the monitor screen. "It's gone! They must have discovered our ruse and found the tracking device. We've been made!"

"Let's spread out," I suggested. "They can't be too far away --- the blip was on the screen when we got on the elevator."

Reyes turned to his officers, "Each of you take the decks on either side of the ship and we'll check the halls. Detain anyone until we can question them."

We were so close to putting our hands on the perps, but it was beginning to look like they had slipped through our fingers again.

With only one more day at sea, we were going to need a break if Lady Justice was to prevail.

As the security officers burst onto the Lower Promenade deck, Luke and Gwen Larson stepped off of the elevator into the Crow's Nest and blended with the passengers having a drink at the bar.

CHAPTER 15

Day #5 at Sea-Cruising the Gulf of Alaska

Our search had been futile. No one was in the halls and the few passengers on the outside deck checked out.

We were disappointed. We thought that we had them cold, but we'd missed them by just a few minutes.

Our conversation at dinner that evening was subdued. Our Alaskan vacation was drawing to a close and our prospects for bringing the perps to justice before we docked at our final port didn't look good.

After dinner, we went to the Showroom Theatre for another wonderful performance by the ship's ensemble.

Up to this point, we had experienced very smooth sailing. The gentle motion of the ship had actually been quite pleasant --- almost like being rocked to sleep each night, but I had noticed, right after supper, that the movement had become much more pronounced. At the end of the performance, I discovered why.

The Captain made a rare appearance onstage and gave us a brief weather report. For the first four days of our voyage, we had been on the Inside Passage with land on both sides of the ship. That fact, along with the calm, sunny weather, had kept the ship's pitching to a minimum. That was all about to change.

We were now sailing the open seas through the Gulf of Alaska and we were about to be engulfed in a rainstorm with buffeting winds and high seas.

The Captain assured us that there was nothing to be concerned about, but with the inclement weather, several precautions were being taken. All outside decks were now off limits and he advised that if anyone was prone to motion sickness, it might be a good time to take preventative measures. With swells ranging from nine to fifteen feet, the ship was definitely going to pitch and roll.

After the show, there was to be a late night dessert buffet around the pool on the Lido Deck.

Under normal circumstances, Ox would have been the first one in line at a dessert buffet, but I could see that the big guy was getting a little green around the gills and I had to admit that I was a bit queasy myself. Nevertheless, the girls didn't want to miss seeing the fancy pastries whipped up by the ship's chefs, so we headed to the Lido Deck.

The Lido was on deck #11 near the top of the ship, and as soon as we stepped off of the elevator we realized that the pitch was much more pronounced. The water was actually being sloshed out of the pool as the ship rocked from side to side.

Under normal circumstances, the sight of chocolate, whipped cream and thick icing is quite alluring, but that night was a different story altogether.

Ox couldn't eat a bite and neither could I.

After the girls had ogled the craftsmanship of the pastry chefs for a few minutes, Ox pleaded, "Can we go now. I think I'm gonna be sick!" I seconded the motion.

The Captain had mentioned that anyone needing motion sickness medication could report to the ship's infirmary. Ox figured that he'd better do just that.

I had anticipated that I might be afflicted if things got rough. I don't do well on rides that go round and round. At amusement parks, I have difficulties on the merry-go-round, and the whirly-gig things leave me staggering, so before we left, I had purchased wristbands with plastic buttons that were supposed to press against the pressure points that control nausea.

Ox and Judy headed to the infirmary and we headed to our cabin where I could slip on my wristbands.

On the way, I noticed that every door exiting to an outside deck had been roped off with bright yellow tape with the words, 'No Admittance'. The Captain hadn't been kidding.

I undressed as quickly as I could and jumped in bed with my bands in place. As I lay there in the dark, the gentle rocking that had lulled me to sleep on previous nights had turned into a roller-coaster ride.

Even with my eyes shut tight, it felt like my head was swimming in circles. Somehow, I drifted off into merciful sleep.

When I awoke, the ship was pitching even

worse than the night before.

I stumbled into the bathroom. In my defense, I was dizzy, the ship was rocking back and forth and I was desperately trying to hold on to the wall with one hand while aiming Mr. Winkie with the other.

Evidently, I didn't accomplish any of that with any degree of success, because when Maggie came in right after, I heard, "WAAAAALT!" That usually means that I missed.

We dressed and knocked on Ox and Judy's door.

Judy was all bright-eyed and bushy-tailed, but I could see that Ox had experienced a rough night.

The girls chatted away as Ox and I followed along behind, holding the walls for support.

Ox normally eats a huge breakfast, but that morning, all he wanted was black coffee. Unfortunately, Judy persuaded him to eat a piece of toast as well.

Like the night before, the motion on Deck #11 was even more pronounced than in our cabin.

The longer we sat there, the greener Ox looked, until finally he resembled the Jolly Green Giant on the vegetable can, only our giant was anything but jolly.

Suddenly, he jumped up from the table and made a beeline to the nearest trashcan where he deposited his morning toast and coffee.

It was hard not to notice the big guy with his head buried in the trash, coughing and gagging, and from the reaction of the other diners, I guessed that some of them had a rough night too.

Several of the unfortunate ones closest to Ox's trashcan clapped their hands to their mouths and desperately sought trashcans of their own.

It appeared that Ox had started an epidemic, and as I listened to the cacophony of intestinal distress, I could feel myself falling victim as well.

Finally, there was nothing left and after a fit of dry heaves, Ox stumbled back to the table. "I think I'd better lay down," he mumbled.

With Ox leaning on Judy and me hanging onto Maggie for support, we staggered out of the Lido Buffet.

It was hard to look at the horrified faces of the other diners as we passed their tables.

For some reason, the girls hadn't fallen victim to the motion sickness and the last thing they wanted to do on their last day at sea was to sit in a dark cabin listening to their guys moaning and groaning.

As Maggie tucked me into bed, she said something about her and Judy going to a presentation of *The Art of Flower Arranging* in the Culinary Arts Center.

At that moment, I really didn't care where they were going as long as I didn't have to go too.

The last thing that I remembered was Maggie kissing me on the forehead and slipping quietly out the door.

Luke and Gwen Larson watched with amusement as the big cop heaved his breakfast into the trashcan.

"The old guy looks like he could puke too," Gwen said.

"Maybe this is our chance for a little payback," Luke said. "Neither of them is going to be much of a handful like that."

"They've cost us our opportunity to get the gold," she replied, "so I wouldn't be opposed to a little payback."

They watched the two couples stagger out of the Lido with the men hanging onto their wives.

"I'll bet they'll be putting the guys to bed and then taking off to some activity," Luke said. "If they do, that'll be our chance."

They followed, but took separate elevators to Deck #6. They waited until the four of them had disappeared into their cabins before returning to their own room. They cracked their door just enough to watch for the wives coming down the hall.

When they passed and turned the corner to the elevators, Luke picked up the door card reader and the two knives they had used to murder the couple in cabin #415.

He handed one of the knives to Gwen. "Let's do this!"

It was just past ten when Maggie and Judy arrived at the Cultural Arts Center. The program was supposed to have started at ten, so they were surprised when they entered the room and the presenter was packing away her arrangements.

"Over already?" Judy asked.

"Never started," the woman replied. "I guess with the rough seas, everyone's laying low. No one showed up."

"So what now?" Judy asked.

Maggie looked at the daily program and her watch. "There's a Thomas Kinkade Art Exhibition that starts at ten-thirty. I'm worried about the guys. We'd just have time to stop by the room and check on them before the exhibit starts."

"Sounds good to me," Judy said. "I've never seen Ox like this. It's like he's a big kid."

"Walt's the same way when he's sick," Maggie replied. "Guys just don't handle sickness like we do."

They took the elevator to Deck #6 and headed down the hall to their rooms.

They were nearly there when Judy stopped short and grabbed Maggie's arm. "My door is ajar --- and so is yours," she whispered.

"Do you think they're up?" Maggie asked.

"Not a chance. Ox could barely move."

"You don't suppose ---?"

"Yeah, I do. Be careful!"

Judy pushed the door open and saw a figure with his arm raised over Ox's still form. She saw the glint of a knife blade reflected in the light from the hallway.

"NOT ON MY HONEYMOON, YOU BASTARD," she yelled and her years of training as a military MP kicked in.

She flew into the room and grabbed the man's arm just as the knife swung toward its target.

The sound of someone yelling startled me from a sound sleep.

When I opened my eyes, I saw a woman's face contorted with hate, holding a knife above her head.

I heard Maggie scream and it jolted me awake just enough to roll to the side just as the woman plunged the knife into the mattress where my body had been a moment before.

The woman pulled the knife from the mattress and raised it to strike again. "Not this time, old man," she hissed.

I grabbed her arm, but in my nausea-weakened condition, I could sense that I would soon be overpowered.

Out of the corner of my eye, I saw something swinging in the air and I wondered if the last thing that I would ever see was a nausea-induced illusion.

Then there was a 'crack' as the swinging thing struck the woman in the side of the head.

She dropped on top of me like a rock just as the hair dryer that Maggie had used like a bolo struck her again.

Maggie pulled the limp body to the floor. "I leave you alone for just a few minutes and I come back and find you cavorting with another woman."

I had to admire the fact that she could crack a joke at a time like that, but then she broke into tears and threw her arms around me.

That was the Maggie that I knew.

CHAPTER 16

Day #6-Seward and the Alaska Railroad

Judy had called Alejandro Reyes on the ship's phone.

Luke and Gwen Larson were just regaining consciousness when Reyes arrived at our cabins. Both were dazed and bleeding from the can of whoop-ass that the girls had laid on them.

"Jesus, Walt, did you have to get that rough?"

"Never laid a finger on them," I said, pointing to Maggie and Judy.

"You gals did all that?" he asked with surprise.

"Nobody messes with our men," Judy said, handing Reyes the two knives. "If we'd have been a minute later they would both have been shish-kabob. I'm betting that these were the murder weapons used in cabin #415."

"So what happens now?" I asked.

"It could get very complicated, I'm afraid," Reyes replied. "The murder victims were American citizens, but they were killed in Canadian waters on board a ship registered to the Netherlands. We're going to have to sort this thing out to see who has jurisdiction. The main thing is that they're not your problem anymore."

"Maybe not," I replied, "but the man that sent them certainly is."

Reyes took the Larson's to the security room

and held them there while he searched their cabin.

When it was all said and done, with the murder weapons, the door card reader and the safe-cracking tool, he had all the evidence that he needed to put them away for life --- or maybe get the needle, depending on who had jurisdiction.

The Larson's were more than willing to co-operate, hoping for leniency, and spilled their guts about the whole scheme that had been cooked up by Louis French.

We now knew for certain who was the mastermind behind the attempted gold heist. What we didn't know was where he was or if he still had his heart set on the gold.

When we were about to leave the security office, Reyes said, "One more thing." He went to his wall safe and pulled out the bag of gold. "Can you get this to the Stewarts for me. My hands are pretty full here and since you have to de-board so early tomorrow, I may not see them again."

"Be glad to," I said, taking the gold, "and thank you for all your help."

"No --- thanks to all of you," he replied. "If it weren't for you, we may never have caught the bastards that killed our passengers."

It was our last night aboard ship.

We enjoyed one last meal with Den and Mukti and left generous tips for each of them as well as our room stewards.

Even though our cruise had been anything but peaceful, having it come to an end was a bittersweet moment.

We all decided to turn in early because of the next day's hectic schedule.

The ship was to dock in Seward at five in the morning, but since there was no International Airport in Seward, we had to take the Alaskan Railroad to Anchorage, spend the night and catch the plane back to Missouri the next day.

The killer was that we had to board the train at six o'clock, which meant that we would have to haul our butts out of bed at four in the morning. The other problem was that all of our luggage, except our carry-ons, had to be in the hallway outside our room by midnight. The stewards would have it loaded aboard the train and we wouldn't see it again until we arrived in Anchorage.

The Stewarts weren't about to let the gold out of their sight for a whole day in an unlocked suitcase, so they had to pack the loot in their carry-on.

By ten o'clock, our bags were packed and stashed in the hall. We tumbled into bed for the last time aboard the ship.

Having nearly been skewered, plus the twenty-four hours of nausea, I was dead tired, but as I lay there with Maggie by my side, I remembered what I said to myself when the Larson's slipped through our fingers. *"We're going to need a break if Lady Justice is to prevail"*.

As I replayed the day's events, I realized that if Ox and I hadn't been barfing up our heels all day, the Larson's might not have tried to kill us, and if it weren't for the cancellation of the flower arranging, Maggie and Judy might have come back to dead husbands.

We had gotten our break, for sure, but who would have figured that it came as a result of fifteen-foot waves out on the high seas.

Then I thought of another guy whose butt had been saved by a high wind on the Red Sea. His name was Moses. I wondered if there was any connection. If so, Lady Justice must have some friends in high places.

Louis French snapped his phone shut in disgust.

He had been calling the Larson's number since four-thirty. With no answer, he could only conclude that the idiots had botched the job --- again --- and worse, they might have even been caught.

They were amateurs and he had no doubt whatsoever that if they were caught, they would sing like canaries to save their own skins.

He had to assume that everyone knew his identity. The old cop and his wife had seen him and taken his picture on Mount Roberts, so that meant that a makeover was in order.

With the Larson's dismal track record on the cruise, he had anticipated the worst and made preparations.

At five-forty five, French purchased a ticket to Anchorage and boarded the Alaskan Railroad with a carry-on that he hoped would end this silly game of cat and mouse once and for all.

The jarring alarm at four in the morning was both a blessing and a curse. I don't do the wee hours of the morning very well, but I was relieved to discover that the ship was no longer pitching and bucking like a rodeo steer.

We showered, dressed and met our friends in the Lido Buffet for one last quick breakfast.

We were cattle-herded once again, as twelve hundred passengers lined up to exit the ship and head for the Alaskan train.

Many, like us, were going the hundred and fourteen miles to Anchorage to catch planes to where ever they called home, while others would travel the four hundred and seventy miles through the mountains and Denali Park to Fairbanks.

Our portion of the trip was to take just over four hours.

The four of us stayed close to the Stewarts and their little suitcase in which they had hidden a fortune in gold. We knew that French was out there somewhere and could strike at any time.

Unlike the White Pass Train, the Alaskan was full sized and much longer. We were herded onto car #2417, the second car from the end.

Also, unlike the White Pass Train, we were encouraged to move from car to car. In fact, they specifically pointed out that there was a lounge car where adult beverages could be purchased and consumed. I was guessing that it was a profit thing.

Surprisingly, the train pulled out of the station right on time and we were on our way to Anchorage, the final leg of our Alaskan journey.

The train track cut through the beautiful Alaskan wilderness, and the tour guide announced exotic places like Resurrection River and Moose Pass as we chugged along.

We even got to see the Spencer Glacier with its wall of ice high on the mountain above the tracks.

I had loaded up on black coffee in the Lido, and since then, the opportunity for potty breaks had been limited.

About an hour into our train ride, the old bladder was sending urgent messages.

One thing that I had noticed about both of the trains was that they jerked and jiggled --- a lot. There was actually no time, except when the train was at a

196

full stop, when I wasn't either holding onto something or letting my body pitch with the movement of the train --- kind of like on a trotting horse.

I excused myself and headed to the lavatory. It was occupied, so I waited, and soon the door swung open and an old gentleman my age stepped out.

"Good luck!" he said as he passed.

When I stepped inside, I noticed right away that his luck had not been so good.

I realized that I was about to accomplish the trifecta of travel urination. I had pee'd on the wall of an airplane that had hit an air pocket while I was in midstream, a ship that had been rolling in stormy seas, and now I was about to initiate the Alaskan Railroad lavatory.

I unzipped, hung on with one hand and aimed with the other, but it just didn't matter. One healthy jerk and my precise calculations were thrown completely out of whack. I had a feeling of dismay mixed with pride as I watched the yellow droplets slide down the wall.

As I zipped up, the thought occurred to me that someone should invent a toilet stabilizer. Maybe I would work on that in my spare time.

When I stepped out, a blue-haired matron was waiting for her turn. I averted my eyes hoping that she wouldn't recognize me later on.

As the door closed, I heard her mutter, "Good Lord!"

Louis French's seat was located two cars ahead of the Stewarts and their cop friends.

He was in the car between his and theirs after making the first of his preparations.

He met one of the conductors coming down the aisle and handed him an envelope and a twenty-dollar bill.

"I wonder if you'd do me a favor?"

The man took the twenty and nodded.

"I'd like you to deliver this note to a Mr. Stewart in car #2417."

"Sure, no problem."

When the conductor had left the car, French moved to his own car and stepped into the lavatory where he slipped on a wig and fastened a moustache above his lip.

Smiling, he took his seat. All hell was about to break loose.

I had returned to my seat and had just picked up a complementary map of downtown Anchorage, when the blue-haired matron came down the aisle.

When she came along side my seat she paused and gave me a glare that would have peeled paint. She didn't say a word, but her, "Harrumph!" conveyed her message very well.

"What was that all about?" Maggie asked.

"Possibly a case of misdirection," I replied, hoping she would drop the subject.

Maggie was about to continue her interrogation when a conductor entered the car.

"Is there a Mr. Stewart aboard?"

Hesitantly, Mark raised his hand.

"A gentleman in the next car asked me to give you this," he said, handing Mark the note.

I didn't even wait to see the contents of the note.

I grabbed the conductor's arm. "Take me to the man that gave you this --- NOW!"

The startled conductor said, "Sure, follow me."

We went to the car where he had received the note and he looked around. "He's not here."

"Then let's try the next car."

After looking through the car, he said apologetically, "Sorry, I just don't see the guy."

I returned and found a very distraught Mark Stewart.

He handed me the note. "He's here!"

The note read:

Mr. Stewart,
We have arrived at a point where you must

decide how much that gold is worth to you.

I have placed a bomb somewhere aboard the train. I will detonate it at exactly ten-thirty if you do not do exactly as I ask, resulting in the deaths of many innocent people as well as you, your wife and your friends.

You will take the suitcase with the gold, place it in the lavatory of the car in front of you and return to your seat.

After you have deposited the gold, remain in your car.

If, at any time before we reach Anchorage, I see you or any of your friends out of your car, I will detonate the bomb.

I hope that your friends will not attempt something foolish. The gold is simply not worth the staggering loss of life that would result.

L. French

"The s.o.b. even had the gall to sign it!" I exclaimed.

I looked at my watch. "Holy crap! It's ten-fifteen!"

"We've been talking while you were away," Ox said. "If French wants Mark to put the gold in the next car, then the bomb has to either be in our car or the one behind us, and we're betting on our car. If the six of us spread out, maybe we can find the thing."

"Five of us," I said. "If we can't find it in time, Mark has to put the gold in the lavatory. We can't risk the lives of the sixty people in this car."

"Agreed!" everyone said.

"Then let's get to it!"

Mark grabbed the suitcase with the gold and stood by the car door while the rest of us looked under and around every seat, causing quite a disturbance among the other passengers.

Naturally, I was the one that drew the seat of the blue-haired lady. "You again! Harrrumph!"

The poor lady didn't realize that in ten minutes none of us might ever pee again.

By the time we had worked our way to the front of the car, it was ten-twenty-five.

"Only one more place to look," Ox said and stepped out on the platform separating the two cars.

There was nothing in plain sight, so we got down on our hands and knees and looked under the metal platform.

"Bingo!" Ox said, as we looked at the brick of C-4 and the detonator attached to the underneath side.

There was a red wire and a blue wire running from the detonator to the C-4.

"Which one shall I pull?" Ox asked as he reached his long arm under the platform.

"How the hell should I know?" I said. "I'm not a bomb expert. We need Judy."

"No time!" he replied. "Now pick one!"

I looked at my watch and if it was right, we had about thirty seconds.

"PICK ONE!" Ox ordered again.

"RED!" I shouted in desperation.

Ox immediately reached for the blue wire and

gave it a jerk.

I closed my eyes and waited for the explosion --- but it didn't come.

"I --- I --- I said 'red'."

"I know," Ox said. "You haven't let me down yet."

In that one moment, three years of calling the wrong coin flip had paid big dividends.

Mentally and emotionally exhausted, we took our seats among the passengers that had no clue that they had nearly been blown to smithereens.

At ten-thirty, Mark Stewart had not deposited the gold in the lavatory.

"What a shame!" French thought. *"Now all of those people will have to die."*

He actually didn't care one way or the other. When the bomb exploded, the train would come to a halt and he would be the first one on the scene to snag the bag of gold from the rubble and no one would be the wiser.

He punched the button on the remote detonator and waited for the concussion of the explosion, but it never came.

He clenched his fists in anger.

"They've escaped again!" he muttered through clenched teeth. "But not next time! I have one more chance at that gold and I will NOT fail!"

CHAPTER 17

Day #7-Anchorage

We had notified the conductor that there was a disabled C-4 bomb attached to the train, and someone had obviously called ahead, because when we pulled into the depot in Anchorage, a bevy of law enforcement types flooded the train.

Naturally, we had a lot of explaining to do and after an hour of intense interrogation, they finally let us go.

Thankfully, the testimony of the conductor and the contents of the note with the bomb threat shifted suspicion away from us.

The mysterious man, that we knew to be Louis French, was never found.

We were transported from the depot to the Westmark Hotel located in the heart of downtown anchorage. At fourteen stories, the hotel, owned coincidently by the Holland-America Cruise Line, was one of the tallest buildings in Anchorage.

We checked in, received our room keys and found our luggage waiting in our rooms just as promised.

By this time, it was almost one in the afternoon and we were starved, so we found a quaint little restaurant overlooking the harbor and enjoyed a lunch of fish and chips.

Downtown Anchorage was a carbon copy of the other Alaskan cities we had visited --- only larger.

Every street surrounding the hotel was filled with jewelry stores, restaurants, bars and novelty shops brimming with tourist knick-knacks inscribed with 'Alaska', in case the weary traveler had forgotten to buy a souvenir for some relative or friend.

We had decided to just roam the streets and soak up our last bit of Alaska.

Poor Mark was reluctant to leave his gold in the hotel room given the fact that Louis French had devised a tool that would get him into most any room with a key card, so he dutifully dragged the wheeled carry-on up and down the streets and in and out of the stores.

We had been up since four that morning, so by six in the evening, we were all pooped.

We found another cutesy restaurant for supper and then decided to call it a day.

Our plane was to leave Anchorage at seven-ten the next morning, which meant that we had to be at the airport by five. In order to do that, we had to catch the bus from the hotel at four-thirty, which meant another morning of hauling our butts out of bed in the middle of the night.

As on the ship, we had to have our bags outside of our hotel room before we went to bed. Someone, in the wee hours of the morning, would take our bags to the appropriate bus.

I was dog-tired when my head hit the pillow. Vacations are fun, but the past two days had been grueling. If we could just get on the plane without further incident, we would be on our way home and in our own beds by the next evening, and I was certainly ready for that.

The alarm buzzed at the ungodly hour of three-thirty.

I staggered to the bathroom with one eye open and the other still glued shut. I can't say for sure, but I might have added to my résumé by christening the wall of the Westmark. Maggie was so out of it that she didn't yelp, so I had no way of knowing one-way or the other.

We met our friends by the elevator at four-fifteen.

We were about to climb on, when Mark's cell phone rang.

"Who could possibly be calling at this hour?" he wondered.

When I saw the look on his face, I knew immediately who it was.

He punched the hands-free key and we all listened.

"Mr. Stewart, this is Louis French. We've never had the pleasure of meeting personally, but I think you know we have something in common --- the desire to possess that gold."

"What do you want?"

"What I want, is for you to drop the carry-on with the gold into the trash receptacle, located behind your bus, just before your bus pulls away. Then you will board your bus and be on your way."

"And if I don't?"

"Your friends were most fortunate on the train to have located my little surprise and even more lucky to have disarmed it. You will not be so fortunate this time. If that gold is not in the trash receptacle when the bus pulls away, you will not make it out of the parking lot --- I promise you that!"

"How do I know that you'll keep your word?"

"Please, Mr. Stewart. I'm not an animal. All I want is the gold. Once it is mine, I have no further use for you. Do we have an understanding?"

"We do," Mark replied.

"Wonderful!" he replied, and hung up.

We just looked at one another in dismay.

"Oh, Lord, not again," Ox moaned. "What's the plan?"

"We need to get down there and take a look at the situation," I replied. "Then we can decide."

When we entered the staging room, a young woman greeted us and checked our names off of a list.

"You are all on bus #102," she stated. "Your bags are already there."

We exited the building and located our bus. Sure enough, our bags, along with the luggage of all the other passengers, was stacked on the sidewalk beside the bus. The trashcan was just where French said that it would be.

"The bomb could be in anyone of those bags," Maggie said. I noted the desperation in her voice.

"Then we'd better get busy," Judy said.

"Won't French be watching us?" Mark asked.

"Probably," Judy replied, but what choice do we have?"

At that moment, a huge van packed with more luggage for another bus pulled up on the sidewalk blocking the view from the hotel to where our luggage was stacked.

We all saw it at the same time.

"NOW!" Ox shouted.

We rushed behind the van and began unzipping all of the suitcases. At that moment, I was thankful that the TSA had outlawed padlocked luggage.

The big van was almost unloaded when Ox shouted, "I've got it!"

We all looked at what he had found.

"Oh, crap!" Judy said, when she had seen the bomb.

"What?"

"This one isn't wired for a remote detonation --- it has a timer!"

Suddenly the meaning of that sunk in.

"So this thing is going to go off whether Mark leaves the gold or not! One way, he gets the gold and we're dead, and the other way he doesn't get the gold and we're dead and he gets his revenge. We're dead either way!"

"Seems that way," Judy said.

"Can we disarm it?"

Judy looked again. "Four wires this time, red, blue, green and white."

Ox shook his head, "With Walt's track record, I was willing to do a 50-50, but I'm not real crazy about one in four odds."

"How much time?" I asked.

"Twenty minutes,"

"I have an idea. This thing is going to go off somewhere and we can't stop it, so let's make sure it goes off where we want it to go off. Mark, where's the carry-on with the gold?"

He handed it to me and I exchanged the gold with the bomb.

The big van was about to pull away.

"As soon as the van moves, put the carry-on in the trash receptacle and the rest of us will board the bus."

The bus pulled out and the Mark did as he had been instructed.

Once the bag had been deposited, he looked around and held his arm up in the air with his middle finger extended.

I hoped that French took that gesture as a sign of defeat and not defiance.

When we were seated, I looked at my watch. In ten minutes, that trashcan would be blown to bits.

We felt the bus move as the driver loaded the last of the luggage and finally we heard the door slam shut.

He climbed aboard and started his little welcome speech. I just hoped that he wouldn't be too long winded.

When we had all been dutifully informed about the safety rules, he took his seat and fired up the big diesel.

We were the last bus to pull away from the curb.

We all breathed a collective sigh of relief when we were at the edge of the parking lot. The bus came to a halt as the driver waited for traffic to clear.

We looked back and saw a lone figure emerge from the shadows and make its way to the trash receptacle.

The figure reached inside and pulled the bag out.

Suddenly, the dark, early morning sky was illuminated and we felt the bus rock from the concussion of the explosion.

Greed and the lust for gold had claimed the life of yet another man.

EPILOGUE

Twenty-two hours later, after two plane changes and long layovers in airport waiting rooms, we were finally in Ox's van, heading home down I-29 with my dad at the wheel.

He had launched into his improbable story of how he and his Social Security posse had gotten the best of would-be killer, Benny Bondell, before the van's wheels had even pulled away from the terminal curb.

Naturally, he went into vivid detail of how he had used Anne, the CPR doll, to lure the unsuspecting Bondell into the trap and save Mary Murphy's hide.

After we had all been duly impressed with his craftiness and cunning, he mentioned the fact that I would need to work something out between the Police Department and the senior center to replace Anne's head that had been blown away in the fracas.

Something to look forward to on my first day back on the job.

As I sat there listening to his rambling narrative, I thought about how we could trump his story with our own tales of hanging off the side of a mountain, being thrown off of a moving train, nearly stabbed to death in our nausea-induced slumber and barely escaping being blown to bits on two separate occasions, but I kept my mouth shut. No need to spoil his moment of glory. There would be plenty of time later to amuse our friends and family with our near-death experiences.

When Ox and Judy had invited us to accompany them on their honeymoon cruise, we all had visions of a peaceful journey on the high seas, indulging ourselves in fine cuisine and marveling at the splendor of our northernmost state, far removed the murder and mayhem that was part of our professional lives back home.

Unfortunately, it wasn't to be, but when it was all said and done, our adventure together was certainly one that none of us would ever forget, and our friends could boast that their honeymoon was one-of-a-kind. More importantly, it strengthened that special bond that exists when you trust another person with your life.

Mark and Amy Stewart made it back to Kansas City with their gold intact, a fact that Mark said would not have happened had there not been our chance meeting in the airport waiting room on the first day of our trip. In the course of our adventure together, we had saved both their lives and their gold, something that Mark vowed that he would always remember.

He told us later that they had decided to use part of that gold to have a bronze statue of John Stewart erected in Skagway as a tribute to that hardy pioneer that had braved the elements and made the six-hundred mile journey to the Yukon gold fields and returned with a bag of gold --- a feat accomplished by just a small percentage of the thousands that tried.

Before our incredible adventure, Mark's great-great grandfather had been just a vague memory of something passed down to him from his own grandfather, but after having actually been where his great-great grandfather had lived and, experienced to a degree, his amazing life, his roots and family heritage took on new meaning to him and had become a source of personal pride.

A few months later, Alfred Quimby, true to his word, sent us a copy of a historical paper that he had published, documenting the amazing discovery of a bag of gold that had been buried for over a century.

Included in that paper was a photo of Ox and me, knee deep in some unknown prospector's grave, removing a metal box. I had to wonder, how many future students of Alaskan history would stumble upon that photo and wonder about the goobers that were digging up some dead guy's final resting place?

In any event, our deed had been recorded in the annals of Alaskan lore, for better or for worse.

Gold!

Among all of the earth's elements, it is the most highly prized even though it has no intrinsic value other that which has been imposed by man himself.

Since the dawn of civilization, the shiny substance has mesmerized humankind. Excavations of Stone Age burial sites indicate that gold was the earliest element collected and treasured by man.

For more than six thousand years, gold has

been symbolic of power, wealth and status.

The ancient Egyptian kings adorned their bodies with gleaming gold and were buried in golden coffins.

While Moses was up on the mountain taking care of business with the Big Guy, Aaron used the forty days and nights he was away to build a golden calf that became an object of worship for the Israelites.

Spanish conquistadors sailed the seven seas in search of cities of gold.

In more recent history, a hundred thousand men and women braved the harsh Alaskan winters and the hardships of a 600-mile journey to lay their hands on the elusive substance.

Throughout history, there have been men and women, like the infamous Soapy Smith and his gang of three hundred con men and cut-throats, who have committed unspeakable acts, driven by their desire to possess the precious metal of others.

We encountered such a trio in Louis French and the Larsons.

Also throughout history, when greedy men possess the power to take that which is not rightfully theirs and tip the scales of justice, other men step forward to balance those scales, as did Frank Reid and his vigilantes in lawless Skagway.

As long as human nature is what it is, there will always be men like Louis French that will skew the scales of justice, and at those times, the call will go out from Lady Justice for someone to step up and right those scales.

My name is Walt Williams and that's why I'm a cop!

John D. Stewart
Prospector, with his poke of gold, stolen by
Slim-Jim Foster and John Bowers

Soapy Smith's Gang of Con Men

Den & Mukti in the Rotterdam Dining Room

Ketchikan, Our first port of call

Totem Bight State Park. Old Man Feeney?

The Author at Mendenhall Glacier

Beautiful Mendenhall Glacier & Lake

Salmon roasting over an Alder wood fire

Author at entrance to a deserted mine

Mount Roberts Tram rising 1,800 feet

Juneau, Alaska from Mount Roberts Tram

Gold Rush Cemetery

Author at Soapy Smith's Grave

Grave of 'Unknown' #1

Grave of 'Unknown' #2

White Pass Train entering tunnel

Train exiting tunnel on return trip

ABOUT THE AUTHOR

Award-winning author, Robert Thornhill, began writing at the age of sixty-six, and in three short years has penned eleven novels in the Lady Justice mystery/comedy series, the seven volume Rainbow Road series of chapter books for children, a cookbook and a mini-autobiography.

The fifth, sixth and seventh novels in his Lady Justice series, *Lady Justice and the Sting, Lady Justice and Dr. Death* and *Lady Justice and the Vigilante* won the Pinnacle Achievement Award from the National Association of Book Entrepreneurs as the best mystery novels for fall of 2011, winter of 2012 and summer of 2012.

Robert holds a master's degree in psychology, but his wit and insight come from his varied occupations including thirty years as a real estate broker.

He lives with his wife, Peg, in Independence, Mo.

LADY JUSTICE TAKES A C.R.A.P.
City Retiree Action Patrol

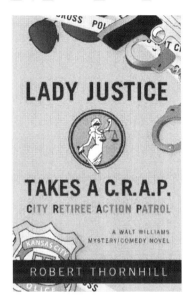

This is where it all began.

See how sixty-five year old Walt Williams became a cop and started the City Retiree Action Patrol.

Meet Maggie, Willie, Mary and the Professor, Walt's sidekicks in all of the Lady Justice novels.

Laugh out loud as Walt and his band of Senior Scrappers capture the Realtor Rapist and take down the Russian Mob.

Visit Bob on the web at http://BooksByBob.com

LADY JUSTICE AND THE LOST TAPES

In *Lady Justice and the Lost Tapes*, Walt and his band of scrappy seniors continue their battle against the forces of evil.

When an entire eastside Kansas City neighborhood is terrorized by the mob, Walt must go undercover to solve the case.

Later, the amazing discovery of a previously unknown recording session of a deceased rock 'n' roll idol stuns the music industry.

Visit bob on the web ay http://BooksByBob.com

LADY JUSTICE GETS LEI'D

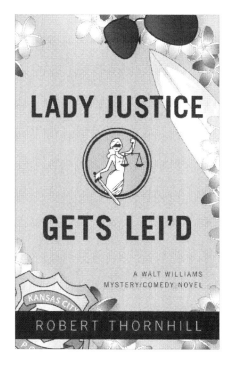

In Lady Justice Gets Lei'd, Walt and Maggie plan a romantic honeymoon on the beautiful Hawaiian Islands, but ancient artifacts discovered in a cave in a dormant volcano and a surprising revelation about Maggie's past, lead our lovers into the hands of Hawaiian zealots.

Visit Bob on the web at http://BooksByBob.com

LADY JUSTICE AND THE
AVENGING ANGELS

Lady Justice has unwittingly entered a religious war.

Who better to fight for her than Walt Williams?

The Avenging Angels believe that it's their job to rain fire and brimstone on Kansas City, their Sodom and Gomorrah.

In this compelling addition to the Lady Justice series, Robert Thornhill brings back all the characters readers have come to love for more hilarity and higher stakes.

You'll laugh and be on the edge of your seat until the big finish.

Don't miss *Lady Justice and the Avenging Angels!*

Visit Bob on the web at http://BooksByBob.com

LADY JUSTICE AND THE STING

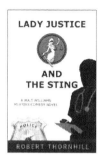

BEST NEW MYSTERY NOVEL ---WINTER 2012

National Association of Book Entrepreneurs

In *Lady Justice and the Sting*, a holistic physician is murdered and Walt becomes entangled in the high-powered world of pharmaceutical giants and corrupt politicians.

Maggie, Ox Willie, Mary and all your favorite characters are back to help Walt bring the criminals to justice in the most unorthodox ways.

A dead-serious mystery with hilarious twists!

Visit Bob on the web at http://BooksByBob.com

LADY JUSTICE AND DR. DEATH

BEST NEW MYSTERY NOVEL --- FALL 2011

National Association of Book Entrepreneurs

In *Lady Justice and Dr. Death*, a series of terminally ill patients are found dead under circumstances that point to a new Dr. Death practicing euthanasia in the Kansas City area.

Walt and his entourage of scrappy seniors are dragged into the 'right-to-die-with-dignity' controversy.

The mystery provides a light-hearted look at this explosive topic and death in general.

You may see end-of-life issues in a whole new light after reading *Lady Justice and Dr. Death*!

Visit Bob on the web at http://BooksByBob.com

LADY JUSTICE AND THE VIGILANTE

BEST NEW MYSTERY NOVEL – SUMMER 2012

NATIONAL ASSOCIATION OF BOOK ENTREPRENEURS

A vigilante is stalking the streets of Kansas City administering his own brand of justice when the justice system fails.

Criminals are being executed right under the noses of the police department.

A new recruit to the City Retiree Action Patrol steps up to help Walt and Ox bring an end to his reign of terror.

But not everyone wants the vigilante stopped. His bold reprisals against the criminal element have inspired the average citizen to take up arms and defend themselves.

As the body count mounts, public opinion is split.

Is it justice or is it murder?

A moral dilemma that will leave you laughing and weeping!

Visit Bob on the web at http://BooksByBob.com

LADY JUSTICE AND THE WATCHERS

Suzanne Collins wrote *The Hunger Games*, Aldous Huxley wrote *Brave New World* and George Orwell wrote *1984*.

All three novels were about dystopian societies of the future.

In *Lady Justice and the Watchers*, Walt sees the world we live in today through the eyes of a group who call themselves 'The Watchers'.

Oscar Levant said that there's a fine line between genius and insanity.

After reading *Lady Justice and the Watchers*, you may realize as Walt did that there's also a fine line separating the life of freedom that we enjoy today and the totalitarian society envisioned in these classic novels.

Quietly and without fanfare, powerful interests have instituted policies that have eroded our privacy, health and individual freedoms.

Is the dystopian society still a thing of the distant future or is it with us now disguised as a wolf in sheep's clothing?

Visit Bob on the web at http://BooksByBob.com

LADY JUSTICE AND THE CANDIDATE

Will American politics always be dominated by the two major political parties or are voters longing for an Independent candidate to challenge the establishment?

Everyone thought that the slate of candidates for the presidential election had been set until Benjamin Franklin Foster came on the scene capturing the hearts of American voters with his message of change and reform.

Powerful interests intent on preserving the status quo with their bought-and-paid-for politicians were determined to take Ben Foster out of the race.

The Secret Service comes up with a quirky plan to protect the Candidate and strike a blow for Lady Justice.

Join Walt on the campaign trail for an adventure full of surprises, mystery, intrigue and laughs!

Visit Bob on the web at http://BooksByBob.com

LADY JUSTICE
AND THE
BOOK CLUB MURDERS

Members of the Midtown Book Club are found murdered.

It is just the beginning of a series of deaths that lead Walt and Ox into the twisted world of a serial killer.

In the late 1960's, the Zodiac Killer claimed to have killed 37 people and was never caught --- the perfect crime.

Oscar Roach, dreamed of being the next serial killer to commit the perfect crime.

He left a calling card with each of his victims --- a mystery novel, resting in their blood-soaked hands.

The media dubbed him 'The Librarian'.

Walt and the Kansas City Police are baffled by the cunning of this vicious killer and fear that he has indeed committed the perfect crime.

Or did he?

Walt and his wacky senior cohorts prove, once again, that life goes on in spite of the carnage around them.

The perfect blend of murder, mayhem and merriment.

Visit Bob on the web at http://BooksByBob.com

WOLVES IN SHEEP'S CLOTHING

In August of 2011, I completed the fifth novel in the *Lady Justice* mystery/comedy series, *Lady Justice And The Sting*.

As I always do, I sent copies of the completed manuscript to several friends and acquaintances for their feedback and comments before sending the manuscript to the publisher.

Since the plot involved a holistic physician, I sent a copy to Dr. Edward Pearson in Florida.

Dr. Pearson loved the premise of the book and the style of writing, particularly as it related to alternative healthcare, natural products and Walt's transformation into a healthier lifestyle.

In subsequent conversations, Dr. Pearson shared that he had been looking for a book that he could share with his patients, colleagues and peers that would spread his message in a format that would capture their imagination and their hearts.

The Sting was very close to what he had been looking for and he made the suggestion that maybe we could work together to produce just the right book.

As I reflected on this idea, I realized that Walt's skirmishes with pharmaceutical companies, corrupt politicians, doctors, nurses, hospitals, bodily afflictions and a healthier lifestyle were not confined to just *The Sting*, but were scattered throughout all six of the *Lady Justice* mystery/comedy novels.

Using *The Sting* as the basis of the new book, I went through the manuscripts of the other five *Lady Justice* novels and pulled out chapters and vignettes that fleshed out the story of Walt's medical adventures.

Thus, *Wolves In Sheep's Clothing* was born.

Dr. Pearson is currently using *Wolves* in conjunction with his New Medicine Foundation to help spread the word about healthcare alternatives.

New Medicine Foundation
Dr. Edward W. Pearson, MD, ABIHM
http://newmedicinefoundation.com

RAINBOW ROAD
CHAPTER BOOKS FOR CHILDREN
AGES 5 – 10

Super Secrets of Rainbow Road

Super Powers of Rainbow Road

Hawaiian Rainbows

Patriotic Rainbows

Sports Heroes of Rainbow Road

Ghosts and Goblins of Rainbow Road

Christmas Crooks of Rainbow Road

For more information, go to http://BooksByBob.com

21112519R00130

Made in the USA
Charleston, SC
08 August 2013